Crossing
Ebenezer
Creek

Also by Tonya Bolden

Finding Family

Tonya Bolden

Crossing Ebenezer Creek

BLOOMSBURY

NEW YORK LONDON OXFORD NEW DELHI SYDNEY

First published in the United States of America in May 2017
by Bloomsbury Children's Books
www.bloomsbury.com

Bloomsbury is a registered trademark of Bloomsbury Publishing Plc

For information about permission to reproduce selections from this book, write to
Permissions, Bloomsbury Children's Books, 1385 Broadway, New York, New York 10018
Bloomsbury books may be purchased for business or promotional use. For information
on bulk purchases please contact Macmillan Corporate and Premium Sales Department
at specialmarkets@macmillan.com

Library of Congress Cataloging-in-Publication Data
Names: Bolden, Tonya, author.
Title: Crossing Ebenezer Creek / by Tonya Bolden.
Description: New York : Bloomsbury, 2017.
Summary: Freed from slavery, Mariah and her young brother, Zeke, join Sherman's march
through Georgia, where Mariah meets a free black named Caleb and dares to imagine the
possibility of true love, but hope can come at a cost.
Identifiers: LCCN 2016037742 (print) | LCCN 2016050232 (e-book)
ISBN 978-1-59990-319-4 (hardcover) | ISBN 978-1-61963-055-0 (e-pub)
Subjects: LCSH: African Americans—Juvenile fiction. | CYAC: African Americans—Fiction. |
Freedmen—Fiction. | Sherman's March to the Sea—Fiction. | United States—History—Civil
War, 1861–1865—Fiction. | Brothers and sisters—Fiction. | Love—Fiction. | BISAC:
JUVENILE FICTION / Historical / United States / Civil War Period (1850–1877). |
JUVENILE FICTION / People & Places / United States / African American. | JUVENILE
FICTION / Family / Siblings.
Classification: LCC PZ7.B635855 Cr 2017 (print) | LCC PZ7.B635855 (e-book) |
DDC [Fic]—dc23
LC record available at https://lccn.loc.gov/2016037742

Book design by Colleen Andrews
Typeset by Westchester Publishing Services
Printed and bound in the U.S.A. by Berryville Graphics Inc., Berryville, Virginia
2 4 6 8 10 9 7 5 3 1

All papers used by Bloomsbury Publishing, Inc., are natural, recyclable products
made from wood grown in well-managed forests. The manufacturing processes
conform to the environmental regulations of the country of origin.

In memory of those sturdy black bridges,
male and female, I was blessed to have as family.

Crossing
Ebenezer
Creek

PROLOGUE

In a southeast Georgia swamp, when a driving rain drenches an early December day, bald cypresses seem to screech, tupelos to shriek, Ebenezer Creek to moan.

Science minds try to explain it away with talk of air flow, wind waves, and such, but others shake their heads. *Not so.* They say it's the ghosts of Ebenezer Creek rising, reeling, wrestling with the wind. Remembering.

Remembering desperate pleas, heartrending screams.

Remembering hope after hope, dream after dream, and—

Mariah, who had dreamed of a long life with Caleb and at least one acre, she first remembers that twelve days before she reached Ebenezer Creek, a hungry hush sent a shiver down her spine.

THEN SHE HEARD THE THUNDER

She dropped the scrub brush, sprang to her feet, peered through the cookhouse window. Sudden quiet too queer.

Yonder in a sweet gum tree, a crowd of crows rose up. They hung in midair for three heartbeats, then swept east.

Something was coming. Good or evil the girl couldn't tell, but she knew it best to bolt.

Lithe and long-legged, she bounded through the back door, raced to a little boy picking up pecans from the ground.

On the outskirts of her mind, she heard a bell tolling frantic, glimpsed others dashing, scattering.

"Come on!" She grabbed the boy's hand. Their hiding place was in the root cellar. A dugout beneath a pile of croker sacks.

Amid the musty smell of red clay, sacks of onions and potatoes, bushels of beets, rutabagas, parsnips, and carrots, she listened for sounds in the distance, for gunfire, for—

Then she heard the thunder—pictured a thousand horses, full gallop.

Hands went quick over the boy's ears when the Big House front door was kicked in.

Next she heard Callie Chaney screaming bloody murder.

Then a thud.

The sound of dust settling ensued, followed by the crash-and-shatter of china and glass.

Voices low, muffled. No way to tell. Outlaws on the prowl? Or was it—

Then came flashbacks of Callie Chaney's scare talk.

"Yankees are monsters!" the woman used to shriek. "Devils! Pure devils!" Wagging a bony finger in her face, Callie Chaney had warned, "You go traipsing off after bluecoat brutes, you won't reach nowhere but dead."

Cellar doors creaked. She clamped a hand over the boy's mouth.

A pistol clicked.

"Anybody down there? Come out now if you know what's good for you!"

The voice was hard, quick. Not one word had a curl or dragged out long. It had to be a Yankee!

Praise God!

The girl had never believed the scare talk. She had prayed for Yankees to come her way ever since the war broke out forty-one months ago. Forty-one long months of huddled, quivering hope.

Battle of Fort Sumter . . . First Manassas . . . Second Manassas . . . Sharpsburg . . . Lincoln's great and mighty Emancipation Proclamation . . . Gettysburg . . . Cold Harbor.

With the others she had been stitching things together from news overheard while tending guests or spied during stolen glances at a *Macon Telegraph* meant for trash.

Days ago word came of Atlanta licked up in flames and how on the heels of the hurt he put on that city, a Union general named Sherman had his army marching southeast.

Let them come by here! the girl prayed every day. Atlanta was more than one hundred miles away from where she was held. When she heard that Yankees had stormed Milledgeville, some thirty miles away, she prayed harder. *Lord, let the Yankees come by here.*

And in the last two days, there was gunfire and smoke from Sandersville. And now—

"Anybody down there? Come out now if you know what's good for you!"

Trusting her gut, she shouted from beneath that pile of croker sacks, "Don't shoot! We coming out!"

RIDDLEVILLE ROAD

When Caleb turned off Riddleville Road and headed for the Big House, he heard a woman's screams and the breaking of things.

Under a canopy of oaks he rode down the long driveway thinking about where he'd start loading first. A half mile back the squad had come across an old colored man who told them what they'd likely find.

At first the man had just stared at Caleb and the thirty or so mounted white men. "Y'all what's left of Sherman's army?" the old man asked, utterly dejected.

Captain Galloway instructed him on how to catch up with a larger force. He also told him that when the squad was done scouting out provisions, it would head for this same force. The man was welcome to travel with them.

The old man, now smiling, eased over to Caleb. "How many in what he call the larger force?" he whispered.

"Thousands," Caleb whispered back.

The old man decided to make tracks for the larger force right then and there. Before he did, he told them about the Chaney place up ahead. "Not what it once was, but she still is wukked and got a top tanner." He then sketched out the place, Big House to barn.

"Is the place for the Union or the Rebellion?" Captain Galloway asked.

"Secesh!" the old man replied. "Two hundred percent and higher. Not a place around here for the Union."

"How many white men on the place up ahead?" Captain Galloway also asked.

"Nary a one I know of now," was the old man's response.

Caleb knew that news of a pro-Rebel place with no white men about ginned up some of the Yankees to go in hog wild, no matter what Captain Galloway said. Not wanting to get caught up in that, as they got closer to the Chaney place Caleb put a little distance between his wagon and the rest of the forage squad, slowing his horses to a trot.

Captain Galloway kept his horse at a canter, shouting out to his men, "Order! Remember, all in order!"

Caleb was almost at the end of the driveway when he brought the buckboard to a stop. He took off his duster, balled it up behind his toolbox, took up the reins again.

"Giddyap!"

Smokehouse . . . corncrib . . . root cellar. Caleb played a guessing game of how many sacks of this and bushels of that he could fit in his wagon. Then he reminded himself to leave room for a person or two. After all, the old man said the Chaney place was still being worked. If any of the colored were of a mind to take their leave, like always Caleb would gladly give them a ride.

Green Eyes

Two scruffy, scraggly bearded soldiers in sky-blue trousers and dark-blue sack coats flanked the root cellar doors. Musket rifles at the ready.

From astride a bay steed, a third white man—crisp, clean-shaven, long, lean—looked down on her and the boy.

"Captain Abel Galloway, United States Army," he boomed, holstering his pistol. "Is the owner of this place for the Union or for the Rebellion?"

From the tone of his voice, the girl sensed the man knew the answer. She took him to be the orderly type. Sounded to her like he was exampling for the scruffy ones.

"Rebellion, sir." She kept her sharp, dark eyes trained on the ground, the boy tight by her side.

"And you have been held in slavery?"

"Yes, sir." The jackknife in her apron pocket got a nervous pat.

"No more!" announced the captain. "No more slavery for you. You now own yourselves."

Something in his voice made her chance a glance up.

The keen-faced captain was smiling. Jet-black hair gleaming. Green eyes sparkling. He could have been singing "Joy to the World" on Christmas Day.

She lowered her eyes as the man continued his say. "By proclamation of President Abraham Lincoln, on the first of January in the year of our Lord 1863, you are free!" He cleared his throat. "And as a member of the United States Army I am obliged to maintain your freedom."

"Thank you, sir." She curtsied, as she had been trained to do not long after learning to walk.

"Always curtsy, no matter their station," said her ma one day while at the loom. "And never look whitefolks in the eye."

"Never let 'em know what you think," her pa had told her on another day while planing pine wood. "Better still, don't even let on you *can* think."

When the girl saw the boy peek out from behind her skirt, she remembered another lesson on survival. Scared stiff that he'd speak, she clamped a hand over his mouth. She was looking past Green Eyes now, wondering about Josie, Jonah, Mordecai, the rest.

"Anyone else in the cellar?" the man asked.

She lowered her eyes again. "No, sir."

"Much food in there?"

"Fair amount." She glanced up, saw him wave the two scruffy ones down into the cellar.

"Remember, Private Sykes, Private Dolan, don't take it all," he said. "Rebel-she though she be, it's not for us to make her starve." With that, off he galloped.

A split second later, little boy in tow, the girl took off for one of the dismal mud-daubed log cabins that bordered the woods. Heart pounding and the words from Green Eyes a song to her soul, she outright wanted to fly. *No more! . . . No more slavery for you . . . You now own yourselves . . . You are free!* At last she was getting away from the Chaney place! At last she was—

But she had a fright when she entered her cabin.

Ladder-back chair overturned. Water jug in pieces on the floor. Cedar trunk lid thrown back.

Thank goodness, the trunk had only been rifled through. Nothing taken. Not her second dress, not the boy's second britches, not other bits of clothing, her sewing things. Safe, too, the pouch of keepsakes.

From a nail on the wall, she grabbed a sling sack and stuffed it with the contents of the trunk. She tried not to tremble.

Just hurry! Hurry! Hurry!

After praying for this day, after planning how she'd pack up quick—she wasn't prepared for the rush-and-roll of emotions, for the trembling.

On she packed while the boy spun in circles smack in the middle of their one small room. Smiling, he flapped his arms every turn or so.

With one sack filled and another begun, the girl let the boy be.

Tin cups. Wooden bowls. Quilt from their bed. Candles from the crate beside it. Bucket by the hearth that *ka-lanked* with fishhooks, weights, a deadfall trap, snares. Last in, the calabash canteens that hung by the door near her cloak.

"We settin' off." She helped the boy into his wool jacket a size too small. "We leavin'." She had told him that this day might come, told him they'd have to move cottontail fast, but she never knew how much he understood.

"Freedoms?" The boy jumped up, yanked his cap from his jacket pocket, and put it cockeyed on his head.

She looked into his big brown eyes, as round as his chestnut face. "That's right, freedoms." She straightened his cap, pulled it down tight on his head. And just then the porch steps creaked. Heart in her mouth, the girl froze.

She didn't breathe easy till she saw who was at the door.

It was freckle-faced Josie, like a big sister. Josie's baby girl, Sarah, was against her bosom and her son, Little Jack, hung on to her skirt. No bundles, no sacks. The girl knew what that meant.

They'd talked about Josie's rock and a hard place many times after her husband, Big Jack, got the hire-out.

"Can't do it." Josie's tears flowed. "Jack's comin' through this. He'll head back here, I know. If we go, he won't never find us. Never."

"But, Josie, are you—"

"Sure. And sure we'll be fine. Will stay in prayer and keep a machete by my side."

Josie's mind was made up, the girl knew. "Till we meet again," she said, trying not to cry as she hugged Josie, kissed baby Sarah, patted Little Jack's cheek.

"Till we meet again," Josie sniffled.

The sling sacks dug into the girl's shoulders as she headed out. She looked around, back into the woods, called out, "Jonah . . . Mordecai . . . Dulcina . . ."

Yankees laughed, cussed, sent up whoops and hollers. Yankees grew louder with her every step.

Stuffing hams into sacks.

Stringing squawking chickens to saddle-flaps.

Corralling horses.

Bringing hogs to a halt with bullets and bayonets.

She stopped at the root cellar, now ringed with sacks, bushel baskets. Tightening her grip on the little boy's hand, the girl searched the faces of Yankees tramping, galloping by. She was sizing them up, waiting for one it felt safe to ask, "What now?"

Rag-and-Bones Belongings

He was drawn to her, like a river to the sea, the minute he saw her emerge from the root cellar.

Caleb was out of earshot but close enough to see how she avoided Captain Galloway's eyes, kept her words few. She was cloaking her strength, just pretending to be simple, he knew. And so protective of the boy, must be her—

Was her man on the place too?

When she spirited away, Caleb had an impulse to go after her, let her know that he would give her a ride. But what if she had hurried to the quarters to get her husband? Besides, he couldn't come up with an excuse for following her. Nothing to load up back there. Anybody who wanted to escape with the Yankees didn't have to be sought out or called for.

Only once had Caleb gone into the quarters to fetch somebody. Back in Sand Town, on that rainy afternoon, when a half-naked little chocolate girl ran to him crying her heart out. Her granny couldn't walk.

Caleb pulled off his jacket, put it on the child, then had her take him to her cabin.

What a wretched hut. Roof leaking. Holes in the walls stuffed with rags. The room reeked of misery.

The girl's granny lay on a pallet. Mouth twisted. Left hand like a claw. Holding his breath against the stench, Caleb lifted her up, bedding and all, carried her to his wagon. Once he got her positioned safely and a blanket over her body, he helped in the little girl with her rag-and-bones belongings.

"You give your granny some water," he said, handing her his canteen. "And you have some, too, if you want." From his pocket he brought out a biscuit from that morning's breakfast, gave her that too. Wide-eyed and willowy, the little girl reminded him of his sister, Lily.

"I'm Caleb. What's your name?"

"Cora Lee," the girl whispered.

About an hour later, when Caleb reached the campground, he discovered that Cora Lee's granny was dead.

"She went up to be with God," said Caleb to Cora Lee. He closed the woman's eyes, pulled the blanket up over her face.

Cora Lee was a fountain of tears, clinging to Caleb with all her might.

"But just think, Cora Lee, up in heaven your granny will be able to walk again, move about free all she wants."

Caleb held Cora Lee until she quieted down to sniffles,

then reached for an empty sack, filled it with some of the day's forage—salt meat, sweet potatoes, corn. He scanned the crowd of colored people already camped. With Cora Lee by the hand and that sack over his shoulder, Caleb headed for the first two young women who struck him as capable. He explained the situation, asked them to take in the girl.

Cora Lee latched onto Caleb again. "Please don't leave me!" she cried out.

"Now, now," said Caleb. "These young ladies are two of the finest in the land. They will take good, good care of you."

"Come here, darlin'," said one of the women, holding out an apple to Cora Lee.

Once the little girl was in the woman's arms, Caleb took his leave and dealt with the corpse. That done, he thought about going back to where those two young women had camped, make sure Cora Lee was settled and all right. In the end Caleb decided against it. No attachments, he told himself.

No attachments, he reminded himself on the Chaney place, after loading some hay from the barn, finding the smokehouse almost empty, and heading for whatever Privates Sykes and Dolan had brought up from the root cellar.

MOON IN THE MIDDLE
OF THE DAY

A two-horse buckboard pulled up. Fella at the reins not one bit familiar. She tried to make sense of him from the moment he leapt from the wagon till he reached whispering distance. He brought to mind sightings of the moon in the middle of the day.

Almost ebony. High cheekbones. Narrow, slanted eyes.

"Your everything?" the stranger asked.

The girl nodded.

He returned to the wagon, rearranged some sacks, stuffed empty ones in a corner of the wagon. He motioned for her and the boy.

She hesitated. Then, sensing no menace, she led the boy over. If she was going to chance it with anyone, who better than one of her own?

He planted the boy in the cushioned-up corner of the wagon.

"You Yank?" the child asked.

The young man smiled. "No, son, I'm no Yank, but my name's Caleb." After a pause, he asked, "And you?"

The boy stared at the air.

"Name's Zeke," said the girl, then added, "Me, I'm Mariah."

Caleb relieved her of her sling sacks. "Well, Mariah, I'll need every inch in the wagon. You sit up front."

"Not yet. Somebody I gotta find. We got a minute, right?"

"Got more than one," Caleb replied.

Mariah took off, then spun around. "Zeke, you stay put, you hear me?"

The others could take care of themselves, bound to come out any minute now. But Dulcina, she might not understand what was going on.

"That's not a bad-looking filly," said a soldier as Mariah dashed by, heading for the quarters.

Running faster, she cupped her hands around her mouth. "Dulcina! Dulcina!" she shouted, hoping to be heard above all the Yankee racket.

Where to look?

Mariah ran to Josie's cabin. "Seen Dulcina?"

Josie shook her head. "But you go on, Mariah, go on to freedom. I'll take care of Dulcina as best I can."

Mariah raced into the woods, looked this way, that. "Dulcina! Dulcina!" In a small clearing she saw a bit of cloth fluttering behind a red cedar.

Mariah tiptoed over. "Dulcina? It's me, Mariah."

Dulcina peeked out from behind the tree. Clearly something about the commotion had registered, for the woman clutched a grimy bundle to her chest. Gently, Mariah took her by the hand.

When Mariah returned to the wagon, she saw that Caleb had it all loaded up. Also that he couldn't contain his shock at the sight of Dulcina. So used to her, Mariah had forgotten that to a stranger Dulcina looked a fright. Red-rimmed, darting eyes. Hair a witchy-wild, silver-streaked mane. And so scrawny.

"Texas?" Dulcina's voice was a scratchy meow. There was so much pleading in her eyes.

"Texas?" she meowed again.

Mariah nodded. If telling the poor thing they were bound for Texas would get her into the wagon . . . "Yes, Dulcina, Texas."

But the wagon was full and up front couldn't hold three. Mariah looked at Caleb. Now her eyes pleaded.

She watched the frown fall from Caleb's face, watched him glance around, grab a couple of sacks, step double quick to the root cellar. He took another look around, dropped the sacks into the hole. In under a minute Dulcina was in the wagon, squeezed between a bushel of rutabagas atop a bushel of carrots and sacks of sweet potatoes. Mariah smiled as Zeke brought out a pecan from his pants pocket and handed it to Dulcina.

*   *   *

When the wagon got going, Mariah's heart began pounding again in jubilee of escaping the Chaney place—but not yet. They had just moved over to wait. Caleb brought the horses to a halt a stone's throw away from the Big House.

Before it two soldiers chewing tobacco were in a lazy lean against a wagon with a helter-skelter of stuff: barrel of whiskey, hogshead of molasses, crates of home-canned peaches and peas, bedding, books, tablecloths, piano stool, chair, small table. Spotting some of her dead master's clothes, Mariah knew they'd even rambled the attic. She figured Jonah had been their guide when he loped through the front door behind another soldier. This one had a small chest under one arm, brass spittoon under the other. After he added his spoils to the helter-skelter wagon, Mariah watched as brawny, barrel-chested Jonah led the soldier over to the camellia bushes.

Must be one of the places Miss Callie had him bury silver, Mariah thought just as Jonah smiled at her like she was a sight for sore eyes, then scowled. Mariah read his mind. To ease it, she nodded at Caleb, cupped the fingers on one hand into an *O*, then rearranged them into a *K* that quickly collapsed.

Jonah jerked his head at the camellia bush, winked, tapped his hawk nose. Mariah knew he was signaling something. But what? Before she could signal him to be clear, Jonah dashed back inside the Big House.

Captain Galloway rode up, eyed the soldiers by the helter-skelter wagon, at the one digging up silver candlesticks, tureens, platters. "No fear of God or man," he muttered.

Mariah tensed up when his eyes moved from the camellias to her.

He smiled.

She stiffened. No white man's smile had ever led to anything good. She was relieved when Green Eyes clip-clopped to the other side of the wagon, whispered something to Caleb, who nodded in reply.

"You Yank?" Zeke piped up.

Mariah looked back. Zeke was staring so hard—too hard—at the white man. "Hush up, Zeke!" she scolded. To the captain, polite as pie, she said, "He meant no disrespect, sir."

"None taken," replied the captain. Then to Zeke, "Yes, son, I'm a Yankee."

"Ma say Yanks gives freedoms!"

Mariah trembled as she watched Zeke's eyes scurry over the white man's pockets then stop. "Where freedoms at?" Again he was looking the captain dead in the face.

"Zeke!" Mariah snapped, then to Captain Galloway, "He means no rudeness, sir. Slow-witted." Mariah forgot to breathe.

"But no less precious in God's sight," said Captain Galloway. He reached into his saddlebag, pulled out a pouch, handed it to Zeke. The boy looked inside, beamed. "Look, Ma!" He pulled out two peppermint sticks. "Freedoms!"

The captain chuckled, Caleb chuckled, Mariah exhaled, and out onto the second-story veranda flew Callie Chaney.

The woman's thin white hair was in disarray, like the rest

of her. Stumbling around, she looked this way and that. "Y'all git back here!"

Mariah faced front, clenched fists pressed in her lap, bile at the back of her throat.

"Mariah!"

No more. No more.

"Mariah!"

No more!

No more head shoved into a chamber pot. No more slaps, kicks. No more brooch pinpricks to her arms. For taking too long to get a fire blazing. For scorching a tablecloth. For being two feet away when Callie Chaney was in a murderous mood.

No more!

No more tongue-lashings taken for Zeke, who left the back door open or tracked in mud. "My fault, Miss Callie," Mariah always said. "Was me."

She wiped her eyes, looked back at Zeke. He was gazing into his bag of peppermint sticks as deeply as Dulcina was staring at her pecan.

"Mordecai! . . . Jonah! . . . Sadie! . . . Sam! . . . Esther! Come back here!" Out of the corner of her eye, Mariah saw Callie Chaney walking in turnarounds now. But at least Mariah knew others had packed up for freedom. In such a state of upset, she was too scared to look around and see for sure.

"Nero!" Callie Chaney called out. "Nero, where you at? Nero, bring the bullwhip!"

More haunting, hellish memories surged up. Mariah

fought back tears. *No!* she told herself. *Only praise God! Only fix your mind on freedom!*

"Mariah! Zeke! Dulcina! Git back here!" Callie Chaney's voice had some trail off to it now. "Y'all only off to perish! To perish, I say!"

Mariah looked up, looked around, saw that she was right. Clutching sacks and bundles, others had gathered around the Yankees.

Then came the sickening sight of a soldier by the helter-skelter wagon mocking Callie Chaney. Sashaying around in a circle, he cried out in a fake falsetto and an exaggerated Southern drawl, "Oh, muh darkies! Where muh darkies? Whatever shall I do without muh darkies! Oh, I *do* declare!"

For Mariah, Callie Chaney's screams were no laughing matter, but hammers at her head. Hard as she tried, she couldn't keep the hounding memories at bay, felt dragged back to that dreadful night when she was twelve and her pa—

No, daughter, git inside . . .

No! Eyes shut tight, Mariah strained to keep her mind on freedom.

And Callie Chaney kept calling out names.

Of people long ago sold, hired out, dead.

Of wily ones who stole off after war broke out.

Of those taking freedom now.

"Mariah!" The old woman wouldn't quit. "I told you . . . them Yanks? Monsters! Pure devils! You'll perish, I say. *Perish!*"

Mariah was about to burst. *May you burn in hell!* she screamed within. *May you burn in hell!*

A bugle brought silence, stillness. Two long minutes later, Mariah heard Caleb giddyup the horses, felt the wagon jostle and bump.

This time it didn't stop after a few yards. It rolled on and on out to Riddleville Road with Mariah yearning for nothing but freedom on her mind.

BITTER

Caleb studied Mariah while her eyes were shut tight against the old crone's shrieks.

Burn scar on her neck.

Tiny gash above her left eye.

He cataloged details that hadn't registered before. Faded but clean russet head wrap. Black cloak and gray homespun dress patched in places with burlap. Half apron frayed. Beat-up brogans too big for her feet. He imagined the toes stuffed with rags.

What happened to her man?

Dead?

Sold?

Did he escape—leaving her and the boy behind?

Seeing Mariah in such a terrible state while they waited to move out cut Caleb to the quick. But he didn't think she'd break. If she had held up this long . . .

Mariah. Strong, proud-sounding name. But then he remembered that passage in Exodus about a place named Marah. "A place of bitter water," Caleb said to himself.

How bitter her days? Caleb speculated on how much hell Mariah had endured, especially with her being such a pretty one. Mahogany. Her dark eyes had a shine like diamonds. Lips a bit pouty. Button nose.

If only they were in a different time, a different place. Far away from war, from hate. She would not be in torment, and he would not be a bystander to her pain. Instead . . .

Sighting Mariah, sizing her up, was prodding Caleb to own up to his loneliness. That frightened him. He didn't understand it. It was all so quick.

Caleb had known plenty of girls. Conveniences, ways to pass the time. He had never put effort into anything close to courting. Whether it was easy ones like Clara or Maggie or husband-hunters like Kate, Caleb never formed attachments. Those girls were around his life but never in it. But now his mind was moored on Mariah.

Pretty girls, smart girls, strong girls. Caleb had known a few who were all three like Mariah. But he had never met anyone like her. The way she was with the boy, the madwoman, such a deep goodness, a goodness he had never really cared about until after that bad business a few months ago when he went out of control.

After he came to his senses and changed his ways, he poured all his energy into helping Yankees help his people and thinking about how he could help them more after the war. To do that he needed to keep away from entanglements, attachments. Mariah had him a bit muddled up. Caleb feared the march was addling his brain.

Wings as Eagles

Yard after yard, the farther away the wagon rolled, the more Mariah's pain and anger ebbed.

Not until they were a long holler from the Chaney place did she open her eyes. She found herself on a narrow road. It snaked between a gully and a field of broom sedge. Afternoon sun had it all aglow as far as she could see.

Mariah looked back to check on Zeke.

Asleep.

Dulcina too.

In a wagon behind, Mordecai. Next to him Jonah, hugging one sack like it was life. A little farther back rode Sadie and her youngest. Walking alongside them, her oldest and her husband, Sam, a large leather bag over his shoulder. Heavy, Mariah knew, with scrapers, awls, lasters, and other tanner's tools. Farther back still was Hannah and Esther with their sprouts.

Jonah was smiling. Mordecai was smiling. So were Sadie and Sam. Esther too.

Eyes skyward, Mariah spotted a golden eagle gliding high. Its wingspan had to be over eight feet.

All creation seemed a new sight.

She followed that golden eagle's flight, remembering her ma's frequent whisper at the end of a hard day of carding wool, spinning, reeling, and still with supper to fix. "Shall renew their strength," Patience would say, getting her second wind. "Shall mount up with wings as eagles."

Now Mariah believed that she could run and run, run a thousand miles and not be weary, that she could walk along roads, up mountains, walk forever and a day—not faint.

She took a deep breath, let herself dream.

Still waters, green pastures, peaceful, merciful place. Even if they had to live in a cave, they'd survive. She knew how to fish and trap. Yes, she and Zeke would be just fine, Mariah decided, as the caravan came to a halt.

At the crossroads up ahead, row after row, four abreast, blue-coats marched by. Row after row after row. After them rolled wagons. Steady on came more rows of soldiers.

The men stepped lively to a peppy drum-and-bugle tune as if their gear—haversack, knapsack, bed roll, poncho, ammunition, and rifles slung over their shoulders—was featherweight.

"My goodness!" Mariah gasped. Couldn't tear her eyes away from all the Yankees marching by. "What a power!" She turned to Caleb. "This the rest of Sherman's army?"

"Some of the rest."

"Some?"

"Lots more, whole lot more." Caleb smiled, pointing west. "Miles thataway, the right wing." Sherman's army had a left wing and right wing, Caleb explained. And each wing had two corps. And mostly they marched in four columns.

Mariah had no idea what Caleb was talking about.

"Each corps has more than ten thousand soldiers," he continued. "We're with the left wing, marching with the Fourteenth Army Corps. Just shy of fourteen thousand men."

Caleb didn't stop there—his speech caught speed with every item.

Each corps, three to four divisions.

Each division, two to three brigades.

Each brigade, three to seven regiments.

Each regiment, ten companies. "On average, that is. Some might have nine, with roughly a hundred men in each. All told, there's more than fifty-five thousand infantrymen and artillerymen."

Mariah frowned. "Infant men?"

"In-fan-tree-men. Foot soldiers. Artillery, they handle the big guns. Each corps also has an artillery brigade."

Mariah's mind was stuck on the number.

"More than *fifty-five thousand*?" That sounded like a world. "Some sight that must be." Mariah ached to be, for a slice of time, that golden eagle gliding high. What she'd give for a sky-high view of General William Tecumseh Sherman's mighty march. Like others, she'd learned his complete name, whispering it sometimes like a prayer. She'd heard others call him Moses.

"And there's General Kilpatrick's cavalrymen—the ones who fight on horseback."

Was there anything about the march that Caleb didn't know?

"Five thousand of them, give or take. Cavalry is there to protect both wings, switching back and forth depending where Rebels harass."

So that makes it about sixty thousand, Mariah thought. *A world indeed!* And she envied Caleb's knowledge. She only had bits and pieces, scraps and rags. He had whole cloth.

"Rebels harass much?"

"In spots. Mostly they sabotage, trying to make the march harder than it needs to be."

Mariah didn't know what sabotage meant, but she guessed it was some kind of devilment. "How do Rebels make the march harder?"

"Chop down trees to clutter up a road. Burn bridges."

"Yankees then have to find another way?"

"Usually the pioneers just get to work."

"Pioneers?"

"Soldiers always near the head of the line of march who are skilled at repairing bridges, clearing roads, cutting side roads through forests. Sometimes there's quicksand, mud, marsh. In those cases, pioneers lay down corduroy roads. Most of the able-bodied colored men who join the march wind up with the pioneers. Some help out the pontoniers."

"The what?"

"I'm sorry. Pontoniers are another class of soldier. In charge of floating bridges called pontoons."

Mariah had never met anybody so talkative with a stranger. And by the time Caleb finished telling her about the twenty-five-hundred wagons, the five-thousand cattle, and what all else Sherman left Atlanta with, Mariah's head was spinning. She eyed him suspiciously. "How you know so much?"

"Captain Galloway mostly."

"One with the green eyes, who gave Zeke the sweets?"

Caleb nodded. "We're waiting to fall in with the second division—"

Mariah chuckled. "You truly have a head for all this soldier business. And numbers."

Caleb looked at her, smiled.

"It's how I keep my mind from becoming mush. Learn and think. Think and learn."

His smile was nice, warming.

And they continued to wait. But not Sadie and Sam, not Hannah, not Esther. Hurrying up to the crossroads with their children in tow, they gesticulated, called out. Mariah couldn't hear their words, but she was pretty sure of their want: the whereabouts of Yankees who passed through Hebron, where they all had kin, kin they were sure had joined Sherman's March.

Mariah soon saw that Sadie and the others met with satisfaction. Smiling wide, they waved good-bye.

Bittersweet.

She couldn't begrudge them seeking family, but as Mariah waved back, a sadness crept over her. Snatches of times past hovered up.

Sharing food.

Doing each other's hair.

Turning castoff clothes into quilts.

Dulcina. They had all chipped in some of their rations and side food after Judge Chaney told Nero to cut Dulcina off. "No use feedin' the wretch. Can't work. Can't be sold. Useless."

And whenever Dulcina went off into the woods for too long, someone was bound to notice, and one or more of them scouted her out, fetched her back. Mariah could see Sadie coaxing Dulcina to eat, Esther struggling to get her to wash, and Sadie trying to pass a comb through her hair. No matter how Dulcina lashed out—pushed the food away, overturned the wash tub, slapped them in the face—Sadie and Esther never gave up on her.

Mariah had a sudden urge to call out to them, jump down from the wagon, rouse Zeke and Dulcina, grab their things, and take off after Sadie and Sam, Hannah, Esther. But then

Mariah glanced back at Jonah and Mordecai, and she decided to stay put. Familiars enough. Facing front, she snuck a look at Caleb. Not a familiar, but something close. Agreeable, though peculiar.

Mariah marveled at the good state of his denim pants, blue-checked shirt, the mustard duster stashed under the seat. Clearly his master hadn't been mean as a hungry bear.

Intriguing too was the toolbox she'd spotted beneath the seat. It had an odd design on the front: like a stack of spinning whorls, with a ram's horn poised on top. All in all, Caleb seemed safe. Something of a comfort too. More comfort—and joy—swept over Mariah when she looked back and sighted two more familiars, the Doubles, striding strong as always, matching as always: black linsey dresses and turbans made from a goldenrod cloth. Mariah jumped down from the wagon.

By the time she reached the Doubles, Mordecai and Jonah were already beside them.

"Bless God," said Chloe, squeezing the breath out of Mariah.

Zoe hugged Mariah hard too.

Mariah filled the Doubles in on Josie and those who had fanned out to find family.

A heavy silence followed, like a boil about to burst.

"Nero?" asked Chloe.

"Hide nor hair," replied Mordecai, ramrod straight. "Not since I saw him scoot up under the Big House."

Mariah sent up a silent hallelujah. No more Chaney place! And no more Nero! The fiend, always lording his power over the rest of them. Too vile to show Dulcina mercy—tying her to a post or tree, taunting her, pelting her with chicken bones, stones, whipping at the air above her head, at the ground beside her feet. And frightening her even more with his devilish laugh, his devilish grin.

Chloe nudged Mariah. Eyes trained on the back of Caleb's head, she asked, "And him?"

"Was with the Yankees who came our way," replied Mariah. "Name's Caleb."

"Y'all sure was talkin' a lot," muttered Jonah.

"About the march. He told me a heap of things about the march."

"Sumpin' 'bout him don't seem right," sneered Jonah. "Seem shifty, like he hidin' sumpin'."

"Who ain't when whitefolks around?" snapped Mordecai. "Seems to me it's a benefit that this Caleb came our way."

"How so?" asked Jonah.

"There's an ease to him," replied Mordecai. "And Mariah just said he has knowledge about the march. And look."

Mariah and the others turned to see Caleb and Captain Galloway talking.

"That white man's manner," continued Mordecai, "suggest they got some common ground."

"That's Captain Galloway," said Mariah.

Jonah snorted. "Any colored man got common ground with a white man gotta be a hazard to the rest of us."

"Jonah, please," said Mariah, patting his arm. "This here's no time to borrow trouble—not on this glorious day! Let us fix our minds on freedom and ready ourselves for new tomorrows!"

More Than a Misty Memory

When Captain Galloway came over and started talking about an idea he had—what a relief! It took Caleb's mind off Mariah.

He had been thinking about the light in her eyes when he told her about the march. A babbling fool is what he felt like. And he couldn't stop wondering what happened to her man. He was about to ask at one point, then had second thoughts. Talked about General Kilpatrick's cavalrymen instead. He was talking so fast—he hoped he hadn't come off as a know-it-all, hoped he hadn't made her feel bad about all the words she didn't know. But then he remembered how she teased him about having a head for soldier business and numbers. She wouldn't have done that if he'd made her feel bad. And now he couldn't decide what was more delightful. Her smile? Her laugh?

The twin women she ran off to meet. Impressive. Big-boned but slender and with great horned owl eyes. Stately.

Tall. Were they kin? Clearly they meant much to Mariah. The way she and the others crowded around—were they figuring out a way to travel together? Or worse, head for a different part of the march like those others did during the halt at the crossroads?

Any minute they'd be falling in. Any minute Caleb would learn if Mariah would be riding with him a little longer or never again. He tried to convince himself that if she came back to the wagon to get the boy and the madwoman, he'd handle it fine. Told himself that by the time they reached the campground—and surely by the time he blew out the candle in his tent that night—Mariah would be nothing more than a misty memory.

When the signal to fall in came, Caleb looked back, saw Mariah heading for his wagon. His heart sank when she climbed into the back, but then his spirit soared when she pulled a quilt out of one of her sacks and placed it over Zeke and Dulcina.

"Captain Galloway gave you some good news?" Mariah asked as she rejoined Caleb in the buckboard.

"Not really. Why?"

"You look like you won a prize or somethin'."

MOVING WOUND

On the move again and traveling a wider road, along with rows and rows of bluecoats, Mariah beheld a growing crowd of people. All shades. All sizes. All ages.

From behind boulders and trees and across fields they came. Doubled up bareback on lank mules, scrawny nags. Squeezed five, six in oxcarts, belongings pressed to chests. Women in worn-out dresses, bundles atop their heads, babies on hips. Men in patched pants and frayed frock coats toting sacks. Some old folks had churn staffs as walking sticks. A few were crumpled up in wheelbarrows and being pushed.

A host of girls and boys skipped.

Hosannas honeyed the air. Hallelujahs to God, hallelujahs to Yankees. Even while savoring sounds of jubilee Mariah couldn't help but liken this exodus to one great moving wound. Like her, they all had scars.

Mariah saw limps—some from accidents, some from

hamstringings, she guessed. Saw cropped ears, cheeks branded with an *R*. Saw forefingers missing first joints.

The sight of a girl about nine leading a big grown man by a rope tied around his waist was a punch in the gut. The man had a dull, vacant stare, the same as Zeke sometimes lapsed into. Mariah had vowed that if she ever got free she'd hunt up a special kind of doctor, get Zeke some help. Looking over her shoulder, she saw him still asleep, like Dulcina. Maybe in freedom she'd find help for her too.

"Girl, you keep looking back like that, you'll get a crick in your neck," Caleb teased. "Rest easy."

Rest easy?

All her life Mariah had lived on tenterhooks, even in her dreams.

Rest easy?

What a freedom that would be! If only the Yankees would whip the Rebels today, tomorrow—soon—so she could get on with having new tomorrows.

But where would that be?

"Where we headed?" she asked. She figured they were more than a mile away from the Chaney place.

"Goal is to make Davisboro before dark."

Mariah had never been to Davisboro but knew it wasn't that far away. "After that?"

"Louisville."

"Then?"

"On to somewhere farther south."

They had just rounded a bend. Mariah fought the impulse to look back on Zeke. "This somewhere place have a name?"

Caleb nodded. "Bound to, but General Sherman keeps that to himself."

"Why's it a secret?"

"Keep Rebels in a scramble."

This didn't sit right with Mariah. Going deeper south was not what she wanted. Up north where slavery had been done away with a long time ago—that's where she wanted to go.

New York, if Mariah had her pick. That was the only place up north she had ever had a small glimpse of thanks to a stained, tattered print, that looked to be torn from a book. It pictured a proper brick building. "New-York African Free-School, No. 2" was written at the bottom. Below that, "Engraved from a drawing taken by P. Reason, a pupil, aged 13 years."

Was "P." for Peter or Paul? Maybe Pip? Mariah had wondered the first time she laid eyes on the picture. Did P. Reason have a sister who had pretty dresses? Did she get to go to school too?

Mariah kept the print tucked inside the old speller hidden beneath a floorboard in her cabin. Some nights after Zeke fell asleep she brought out the book, gazed at the print.

Daydreaming on freedom, Mariah could never envision the journey once she got away from the Chaney place. Couldn't imagine the world beyond. Kneading dough in the cookhouse, beating a rug out back, staring at P. Reason's school—Mariah sometimes conjured up a flying carpet at the end of Riddleville

Road. A flying carpet that would take her high up and away to New York, where more good fortune would follow: work and a place to stay in one of the buildings on either side of African Free-School No. 2.

But there was no flying carpet, and the march was heading south.

She glanced at Caleb. He looked relaxed. That calmed Mariah's mind. A bit. Had her trying to convince herself that General Sherman's somewhere place would be safe.

Mariah turned to Caleb with a half smile. "We jus' have to trust the Yankees, right?"

"I trust God and my gut. And Captain Galloway, I trust him."

"He's a kind one?"

Caleb nodded. "More than kind. He's good. Been strong against slavery since he was a boy."

"Abolition man."

"Two hundred percent. More than a few of them on the march."

More than a few of them? What an odd thing to say.

"There's General Oliver O. Howard," Caleb continued. "He heads up the right wing. Like Galloway, strong Christian. They call him Old Prayer Book." After a pause, Caleb added, "There's Sergeant Hoffmann in the company we're with. There's—"

"Ain't they all?"

"Ain't they all what?"

"Ain't all Yankees abolition men?"

Caleb shook his head.

Mariah frowned. "But they freein' us."

Caleb had a funny look on his face.

Mariah became more anxious. "I know about Lincoln's proclamation. And I won't ever forget what Captain Galloway said to me, 'No more slavery!'" After a pause, Mariah added, "They really are freein' us, right?"

Caleb faced her. "Freedom is real, Mariah," he replied. "Don't fret yourself."

Mariah sensed that Caleb was taking her measure. She also sensed that he was holding something back. "What is it, Caleb?"

"I hate to be the bearer of bad news, but the thing is . . ."

"What?"

"Truth is, lots of Yankees don't really care what happens to us."

Mariah's eyes narrowed.

"Many look on colored the way they do cattle. Freeing colored is the same as hauling off Rebel livestock and crops, same as tearing up Rebel railroad tracks, burning down Rebel buildings. Whatever means hell and a mess for Rebels, whatever makes them cry mercy, that's what the Yankees will do."

Mercy. The word triggered another horrible memory, picked at a scab.

Mercy. She'd known precious little of that.

Mercy! She saw herself at the feet of a figure head to toe in black, beginning with a veil. Saw herself a bundle of snot and tears, pleading for mercy.

No more, no more! Mariah pushed back against that memory. She looked up, took a deep breath, fixed her mind on freedom and the mercy at hand. Maybe all Yankees weren't abolition men, maybe many saw colored as cattle. Right then, right there, that didn't matter none to her. Prayer had been answered! Yankees had come her way! Being in that wagon *free*—that was a mercy for the ages! And anybody out to make the likes of Callie Chaney cry mercy was all right with Mariah.

"We heard how they burned Atlanta to the ground."

"Not the whole city, but plenty," said Caleb, suddenly solemn. "Railroad tracks, locomotives, train cars, round-houses, bridges, machine shops, mills. Some blown up. Some burned." Caleb tightened his grip on the reins. "Pillars of fire everywhere."

Mariah felt a chill. She rubbed her arms. "Learned all that from Captain Galloway?"

Eyes on the road, Caleb shook his head. "Lived it."

Caleb's jaw tightened. Mariah wondered what else he was holding back.

Dulcina stirred, mumbled. Not "Texas," just gibberish.

Caleb glanced over his shoulder. "Her name again?"

"Dulcina."

"Always like this?"

Mariah shook her head. "Not before Judge Chaney sold her husband and their boys."

"Judge Chaney?"

"Who owned us."

"I saw only the old woman."

"His wife, Miss Callie. Judge died a few years back." Again Mariah pushed back against memory. After a swallow, she unwrapped the rest of Dulcina's story.

She explained that the judge sold Dulcina's husband, Joe, and sons, Fred and Bunny, to clear up gambling debts. "Not his, but the son, Master Robert." Mariah paused. "Had they been sold to somebody near . . . but they were carried off far."

"Texas?" Caleb asked.

Mariah nodded. "So we heard. And Dulcina, she couldn't bear up. Mind went loose."

Wagon wheels and horses' hooves did the only talking for a while.

"Master Robert reformed himself for a time. But after the judge died, he went back to his mess." Mariah's eyes latched onto a stand of dogwoods, bare to the bone, branches uplifted in worship, fingertips bearing shiny red drupes. "More got sold," Mariah continued. "Didn't stop till Master Robert got killed last summer."

"In a battle?"

"No, in a street in Milledgeville. Shot over some woman."

Gingerly, Caleb asked, "Your husband, he was among the sold?"

Mariah shook her head.

"Hired out?"

Again, Mariah shook her head.

"Did he—?"

"Never had no husband." Mariah was bewildered until she caught Caleb's drift. "Zeke ain't my son."

Caleb rubbed his chin, frowned. "But I heard him call you Ma."

"He's not yet mastered my name. Zeke's my brother."

By then, Caleb was pulling into a meadow bordered by a grove of longleaf pine.

Stroking the Scrub Oak

Hordes of Yankees had already made camp. Arms stacked. Tents pitched. A thousand campfires crackled.

The wagon rolled on, horses in a four-beat gait.

Caleb looked out over all the people, in small and large clusters, making camps in the meadow some distance from the soldiers. Familiar scene. Day after day he'd seen families and flung-together folks, without much talk, with no ado, fall into timeworn routines. Certain ones minded little ones. Others headed for the stream with pots and buckets or into the woods with hatchets and machetes.

Caleb brought the horses to halt by a scrub oak. "This looks a good spot."

By the time Caleb reached the other side of the wagon to help Mariah down, her feet were already on the ground and she was heading for Zeke.

"I'll tend to him," said Caleb. "You take care of Dulcina."

He picked up Zeke and planted him by the scrub oak, then watched as Mariah gave Dulcina a gentle shake.

Dulcina sat bolt upright, looking like her brain was in bedlam. She hauled off and slapped Mariah.

"What in the—" Caleb headed over.

Mariah waved him off. "No! It's fine. I'm fine." She rubbed the left side of her face. "Just one of her upsets."

"Better let me see to her."

"No, Caleb, really, I can handle her."

Caleb wasn't about to leave Mariah's side. He looked from her to Dulcina, saw a calm come over both. He walked with Mariah as she led Dulcina over to Zeke, who was rolling a peppermint stick between two fingers. Not until Dulcina was seated on the ground did Caleb return to the wagon to get their things, even Dulcina's grimy bundle.

"Much obliged," said Mariah.

"Not at all." Caleb was still worried about Mariah. "She in need of restraints?"

"No, she'll be fine."

"You can handle her and the boy by yourself?"

"Won't be by myself," replied Mariah. "Here come my people."

Caleb turned around and saw the old man, the young man, and bringing up the rear, the twin women, heading their way.

Caleb tipped his hat. "I best be on my way now, but—"

"You leavin' for good?"

Not if I can help it, thought Caleb.

"Just wanted to know if . . . if you leavin' . . . for good, for if so—want to give a proper thanks. For the ride, all the aid."

One horse nickered, the other neighed as Caleb watched Mariah fidget. "Need to parcel out some things then take the remainder to the commissary officer," he explained. "I'll be back."

SAVORING THE SIGHT

Mariah had no idea what a commissary officer was, and she
didn't care. Caleb was coming back. Nice. Warming like his
smile. As she watched him walk away, she found herself savoring the sight of his shoulders. And the way he walked. Like
he knew how to make his way in the world. She wondered—

No, woolgathering wouldn't do. She needed to get her
bearings.

Mariah reckoned the time by the sky. Took in the height
of longleaf pines. Her mouth watered as the aroma of beef
stewed, roasted, of pork being fried, wafted her way from
where soldiers camped. Her stomach growled. During the
ride she'd felt peckish, but now it was as if she hadn't eaten a
morsel in days.

Mariah saw herself in their cabin after sundown, slicing
fatback to flavor a pot of greens, heating the skillet to a sizzle

for corn pone. Big dinners at the Big House before the war came to mind next. Sadie in commotion, fussing over the feast. Baked ham with brown sugar glaze, spiked with cloves. Turkey oozing oyster dressing. Corn soufflé, potato soufflé, creamed peas, candied carrots. Mariah smiled at memories of Sadie slipping her a bit of berry cobbler or sweet potato pie for Zeke.

The cracklin' bread she'd packed—how long would she have to make it last, Mariah wondered as she went to help the Doubles bring their sacks and bundles over to the scrub oak tree. One of Miss Chloe's was bound to hold hyssop, pennyroyal, dandelion, and bundles of other roots and herbs. Bark too. And Mariah was pretty sure that Miss Zoe wouldn't have come away without at least one cast-iron pot, skillet, and some cooking utensils.

"I'll go for water," said Mariah after everybody got settled, then to Jonah, "You'll see to firewood?"

"Yup," Jonah replied.

"I'll get to work on a couple of lean-tos," said Mordecai.

"Zoe packed some ham, biscuits," said Chloe.

"You'll find some cracklin' bread in one of my sacks," said Mariah as she headed for the stream, a bucket in each hand and a calabash canteen around her neck.

Along the way Mariah found herself smiling. Smiling at the people she passed. Smiling at the trees. At freedom. Smiling, too, at the thought of Caleb coming back.

LEARN THEIR STORIES

"One chicken per dozen or so, one sweet potato each."

That's what Caleb heard Captain Galloway tell Privates Sykes and Dolan as he drew near.

"Colored people are not the only ones in need," the captain had said earlier. "My men are needy too. In need of seeing how the world should be. In need of seeing how much they don't see . . . the family of man."

Captain Galloway was the most unusual white man Caleb had ever met. He was leery at first, suspected the captain's kindness was a cover for a coming trick. After traveling with him for thirty miles, Caleb was convinced that the captain was genuine.

Days back, while they supped together, before he knew what came over him Caleb told Captain Galloway about his life in Atlanta. About what a rascal he had been. About those days of hosting evil. How close he came to murder. Then about his turnaround.

"Appreciate it, sir, if you keep it all to yourself," Caleb had asked.

"You have my word," Captain Galloway pledged, stirring his three-legged cast-iron pot. Then he shared his own journey to faith. He also told Caleb about his mother's side of the family. "Two plantations on Maryland's Eastern Shore. At the start of the war, they had over a hundred slaves."

"Your father from the South too?"

"No. New York born and bred." After a pause, Captain Galloway said, "I'm sorry, Caleb. So very sorry."

"You can't help what your mother's people did."

Captain ladled a helping of beef stew into Caleb's mucket. "Not talking about just them."

Caleb thought he saw tears in his eyes.

"I thought I knew how evil slavery was," the captain continued. "Reading about it doesn't tell the half. Hearing Douglass or Brown or some other soul fortunate to have escaped, even that doesn't truly capture it, because when such people are giving lectures and writing their books, they've had some time to heal. But on this march I see hundreds, thousands who aren't even at the start of that." After a pause the captain said again, "I'm sorry, Caleb, so sorry."

That was the first time Caleb ever heard a white person apologize to a colored for anything. When the stagecoach ran over Keziah Turner's lad, there had been no sorry. When

Jeremiah Auld falsely accused Mac Purdy of stealing horses—
and got him whipped—there had been no sorry. For all that
Caleb's father had endured—no sorry. And when Caleb went
after the man who destroyed his sister, he knew there'd be no
sorry from him. By then Caleb hated them all. Since then, he
had worked hard to conquer hate, but there were moments on
the march when bitterness got the best of him. Captain Galloway's sorry helped. That and the man's efforts to make a
mission field of the march, aiming to convert as many of his
men as he could to see the world as he did. To see colored
people as he did.

A time or two Caleb sat in on one of the captain's talks
where he handed out tracts about slavery. And now he watched
him put another plan into action, starting with Privates
Sykes and Dolan. "They say they are Christians. I want to
help them prove it."

Captain Galloway had the privates load a wagon with food,
then said, "Twelve. Get them in groups of twelve or so. They
might be one family, might be two, possibly more. If there's
any bunching up to do, let them know it's only for purposes
of provisions. Once the meal is done they can belong as they
wish."

Private Dolan, slack jawed and rangy, ran a hand through
his tousled blond hair. "I should get our rifles?"

Galloway peered at him. "Rifles?"

"To round them up?"

"Round up who?"

"The nig—the colored people."

Caleb could see the captain struggling not to lose his temper. That was one of their bonds. Both had worked hard to tame their tempers.

"Private Dolan, there is no rounding up!" said the captain. "You simply move out across the field, call them over, and explain things in a Christian but firm way." He looked from Dolan to Sykes. "Understood?"

"Yes, sir!" said the privates in unison.

"Then you hand out the food," Galloway continued. "As I said, one chicken per dozen or so, one sweet potato each."

Caleb had seen the captain hand out more than chickens and potatoes. He guessed he wanted to keep Sykes and Dolan's first time simple.

Sykes, stout and ruddy, scratched his head.

"Is there a problem, Private Sykes?" asked Captain Galloway.

"No, sir. Well, sir, I was just—it sounds like we'll be serving the . . . them."

Caleb looked down, tried not to laugh.

"You will be serving your Lord and Savior," said Captain Galloway.

When Caleb looked up, he saw the two young men heading off on their mission.

"And one more thing," Captain Galloway called out.

The privates about-faced.

"Talk to them," said the captain.

"About what, sir?" asked Private Dolan.

"About anything that will allow you to learn their sto-ries." The captain pushed his slouch hat over his eyes as he watched the privates cross the field, park, and wave people over.

The people just looked at them. The privates waved again.

"Food, we bring you food," hollered Private Dolan. "In the name of our Lord and Savior, Jesus Christ!"

Caleb drew up beside Captain Galloway. "Good work, sir."

"There's hope for them yet," said the captain.

"Looks like it."

"Sup with me tonight?"

"No, sir. Some business I need to tend to."

Copper-Skinned Boy Was Ben

Mariah returned with another two buckets of water and another full calabash canteen around her neck. During her first trip back she saw Zoe getting food from the two scruffy ones, and so she knew they could save her cracklin' bread and Zoe's ham and biscuits for tomorrow. And it wouldn't be long before her hunger was gone.

Zoe was about through dressing the chicken, Mordecai about done building one lean-to. Zeke and Dulcina still sat by the scrub oak, behind a fortress of sacks and bundles. Both looked like they had not a care in the world. And to Mariah's eyes, that was a good thing.

She set the buckets down, stretched her back, took the calabash canteen from around her neck, then headed for Zeke and Dulcina. As she gave them sips of water, Mariah tried to get a read on the folks they wound up with for supper.

Old man, olive-skinned, rigging up a spit.

Old woman, nutmeg, impish eyes, keeping the fire.

A brown-skinned girl, younger than Mariah and shy-looking, just sat there fumbling with her fingers.

About Josie's age, Mariah reckoned of the short, dark-skinned, bowlegged woman in the family way. The rail-thin pop-eyed girl on her lap was maybe three.

"I'll make her some sage tea," Mariah heard Chloe tell the woman after checking the child's glands.

Before long the chicken was on the spit, the sweet potatoes in the ashes. While they all readied for supper—brought out tin plates, cups, gourd dippers—there was soft talk, acquaintance making.

Mariah learned that the old man was Hosea and the old woman his wife, Hagar. She told everybody that the timid one was Miriam and that they'd taken her in after they saw her join the march by herself. The way Miriam shied away from her gaze, Mariah wondered if the girl was mute. Or had her mind gone loose like Dulcina's?

"Name's Rachel," said the pregnant woman. "And this my daughter, Rose."

"Like Miriam," said Hagar, "when we seen Rachel and Rose with only theyselves, we welcome them in, too. A few miles later he come along on a wall-eyed pony." Hagar pointed at the copper-skinned boy who had helped Jonah fetch firewood. The copper-skinned boy was Ben.

More than once during supper, with the children given mostly the stray parts—liver, gizzard, heart, neck, feet—Mariah saw Zeke stare at Ben's right hand, at the forefinger with the first joint gone. Each time Mariah steered her brother's attention to something else, like sucking the chicken neck clean.

Every now and then Mariah glanced around the campground.

Was Caleb really coming back?

General Reb

Caleb came back with a dinted coffee pot, a couple of large tin cups, canned peaches, hardtack, a bar of soap, blankets, bedsheets, brocade draperies, a wedge tent.

He nodded, said "Pleased to meet you" as Mariah introduced him to Mordecai, the Doubles, Jonah. After he put the basket of goods on the ground he took out something wrapped in a coarse linen towel, handed it to Mariah.

Caleb watched her unwrap the package and light up over an almost new pair of lace-up boots.

In no time at all Mariah had her beat-up brogans off and her new shoes on.

A fine fit, Caleb could see.

"Mighty grateful," said Mariah.

It did Caleb's heart good to see Mariah happy for at least a moment in time. And he pretended not to notice Jonah's dirty looks. Instead Caleb turned his attention to Zoe inspecting the hardtack. She sniffed it, gave it a titmouse taste, arched an eyebrow.

"For emergency," Caleb explained. "In case there's no time to cook or weather won't permit. Kept dry, hardtack will last a hundred years."

Now that he got a long look at them Caleb was convinced that the only way to tell the Doubles apart was by their duties and dispositions. One not prone to much chit-chat, the other sunnier. The way the silent one took charge of the peaches and the hardtack, Caleb figured she was a cook. The way the other one was grinding up some bark and herbs with a mortar and pestle—a healer. *But clearly no miracle worker,* he thought as he glanced at Zeke sitting in Mariah's lap staring into another world and Dulcina picking lint that wasn't there from her grimy bundle.

Watching Mordecai and Jonah floor two lean-tos with pine boughs, Caleb guessed from their bearings that one had been a butler or coachman, the other a field worker—and Jonah seemed to be spoiling for a fight. *Let it not come to that,* Caleb said to himself, then went to work on the tent. A tight fit for the women and Zeke, but surely they'd rest better.

"There are pickets posted around the campground, on guard all night," Caleb explained. He told them about the bugle call for lights out, the bugle call for rise.

Caleb saw Mariah watching his every move. How he laid out the canvas, where he drove the stakes, joined the poles, assembled them. When done, he handed her the mallet. "Come morning I'll show you the quickest way to strike."

Caleb sat down on his haunches, lowered his voice. "I'm sure I don't have to tell y'all about the need to keep alert and watchful. All along the march we've run into Rebel sharpshooters. Mostly if they ambush they go after Yankees. But still . . ." He paused as Zoe arched an eyebrow and Chloe, Mordecai, and Mariah leaned in. Jonah tossed pine knots on the fire.

"Rebels ain't the only ones you need to watch out for," continued Caleb. "You especially need to keep top eye open for the commander of the corps we're with. He hates us and got not one quarrel with slavery. Believes it's what we fit for. Some soldiers call him General Reb—but only behind his back."

Caleb paused to let it all sink in.

"I told them what you said about us bein' like cattle to some Yankees," whispered Mariah. "Now you say some Yankees favor slavery?"

Caleb nodded, then told them about one of General Reb's recent orders. "He complained about there being too many what he called 'useless negroes' on the march, that our people eat food much needed by the troops and take up too much space in the wagons."

"'Useless negroes'?" Mordecai frowned, rubbed his bald pate.

Caleb nodded. "And what General Reb decreed is that no wagons are to carry colored people or their belongings. Except for ones serving certain officers, no colored are allowed to ride on horse or mule."

"How will we know this, this General Reb?" asked Mariah.

"First off, generals have stars on their shoulder boards, and General—"

"Shoulder boards?" asked Mariah.

Caleb tapped one of his shoulders. "Patches on each," he explained. "General Reb, he has two stars. His face fits his spirit. On the ghoulish side. Bushy mustache and beard. Hangdog pasty face. Cold blue eyes. Right deadly."

"What kind of horse he ride?" asked Mariah.

"I've seen him on a dark bay, a sorrel, but mostly on a dapple gray." Caleb looked over his shoulder, then back at the group. "Adding salt to the wound is his real name. You'll never guess." When no one did, Caleb said, "Jefferson Davis."

"What that cuss have to do with General Reb?" asked Mordecai.

"No, that *is* General Reb's name. Jefferson Davis."

"You joshin'!" Mariah gasped.

"Not one bit," said Caleb.

"Jefferson . . . Davis." Mariah frowned, shaking her head in consternation that this hateful Union general had the same name as the president of the Confederacy.

Caleb rose, looked at Hagar and Hosea's band making their campsite some ten yards away. Didn't recall seeing them before. "Put it on the grapevine for everybody to be on the

lookout for General Reb. Don't let him catch any colored riding in a wagon or on a horse or mule. I also advise not letting
him catch sight of any of us receiving kindness from a Yankee." With that, Caleb bid them all good night. Even Jonah.

At the Cusp of Dawn

A part of her walked with him until Caleb was out of sight, the outline of his body blended into the night.

Then duty called.

Mariah had to get Zeke and Dulcina settled in the tent and off to sleep. Zeke under a blanket, Dulcina under the drapes. That done, she joined the others around the fire, only half-listening to their talk. She reckoned Caleb was two, maybe three years older than her, and she wondered what manner of man he was.

She remained around that fire after the Doubles said their good night, after Mordecai stretched out his long bones in his lean-to. The last thing Mariah wanted to do was sleep. And she knew that if she stayed up, Jonah wouldn't head for his lean-to anytime soon.

Mariah tightened her cloak around her.

"Warm enough?" asked Jonah.

Eyes on the fire, she nodded, knowing Jonah would lay on more firewood anyway, which he did.

In the distance somebody blew a few notes on a harmonica, eased into a lilting, yet mildly mournful tune.

"Sure is a fine night," said Jonah.

Mariah gave him a quick smile.

Jonah cleared his throat. "Our long wait is over."

"Moments I can't believe it's true, fear I'm in a long dream." Mariah looked around at the night.

Couples cuddled up.

Mothers rocked babies.

She imagined bobwhite quail and timberdoodles nestled in the woods.

Jonah leaned in. "What you thinkin'?"

Mariah pictured whitetail deer padding close by. "About freedom."

"But you seem so . . . solemnlike. Ain't you gladhappy?" Jonah pulled his cap down tighter on his head.

"Gladhappy?" Mariah stretched her arms, her back. "Gladhappy is . . . a hambone to flavor soup, new cloth at Christmas. Those the sort of things that make for gladhappy." She saw Jonah turn glum. Had she accidentally given him the look?

"It's a look that tells me you think I'm thick," he had once grumbled. "Like when you got on me about lessons."

How well Mariah remembered that argument. Her pushing Jonah to learn his letters. Him saying there was no need for both of them to be able to read and write. Her pretending she didn't catch his drift.

Jonah had called it quits after learning the alphabet and how to spell a few simple words like dog, cat, and okay. "Can't see how readin' come in handy if you hungry or freezin' to death."

Mariah knew that if Jonah had to choose between hunger and cold, he'd choose hunger. So great was his fear of the cold, a fear that came on him after that day they were helping Sadie in the cookhouse. Sadie sent Jonah to the Big House with a tray of groundnut brittle, meant for white children soon to come caroling. After he laid the tray on the front hall table, even though Sadie had said she had set some aside for him, Jonah couldn't resist temptation. He snuck a piece of brittle into his pocket, and Judge Chaney saw him.

No shoes, no stockings. No coat, no cap. In just his tow cloth shirt Jonah was made to stand out back for what seemed like hours, shivering so on that cold and windy Christmas Eve. Little Mariah had wondered if his tears would freeze.

Jonah added sticks to the fire.

"This is beyond gladhappy, Jonah," Mariah said. "Bein' here right now, breathin' in freedom . . . Gladhappy don't strike me as a big enough word." Then she rose.

"Turnin' in?"

Mariah shook her head, tightened her cloak around her.

"Well, where you off to?" Jonah rose too.

"To myself." Mariah smiled, patting Jonah's arm. "Don't worry. Not far."

By the scattering of campfires Mariah stepped gingerly to a clear stretch of ground. Stars, numberless, were beginning to shine.

Gazing up, Mariah whispered, "Thank you, Lord."

For Jonah—always a help. Skinning rabbits and possums she trapped. In the winter daubing chinks in the cabins along with collecting cow chips and kindling overmuch so all in the quarter could keep warm.

She thanked the Almighty for Mordecai too. *So wise.* He'd picked up where her ma and pa had left off on how to read people and such. *And so kind.* Warning her when Miss Callie was in a tempest. Sparing her from having to carry things up to Master Roberts's room when the miscreant was in it. "I'll take it up," he'd say if Miss Callie wasn't about.

As for the Doubles—*like mothers to me.* When Chloe was called to the sick room on the Chaney place, she could make a sweat seem a fever, a sprain a break, so a body got more time off work. Some Sundays Zoe came with a basket of ginger cakes or other treats. Hidden under the treats, now and then, was an item a member of the Melrose family had tossed aside. Blue-back speller. A reader. Half-used copy book. Cracked slate. Lump of chalk. That print of the African Free-School No. 2 in New York.

Mariah eased down onto the ground, pulled her knees up, and draped her arms around her legs. She rubbed a hand over the top of her boots.

And Caleb. She added him to her list of blessings.

Mariah went misty-eyed thinking about her brother. Zeke's simple cheer had been her only real joy these last few years. Then she saw herself over the years, praying as she polished the parlor floor, lit fires, made beds, cleaned grates, washed chamber pots, milked cows, churned butter. Saw herself praying as she stood, paced, knelt, rocked before her hearth. All those days, weeks, months, years of pleading. For a weakening of the Chaney wrath. All those days, weeks, months, years of pleading. For strength of body. For her mind not to go loose.

Not now. On this night so divine, Mariah did no pleading. The only thing on her heart was gratitude.

But she did have one request.

She wanted to stay awake, wanted to see what freedom looked like, felt like at midnight, then at the cusp of dawn.

CAMPED AT DAVISBORO

"Sun., Nov. 27th, 1864," Caleb wrote in the upper right-hand corner of the page. He chided himself for failing to write for the last few days, wanted to play catch-up.

"Milledgeville is behind us. It is a bit simple for a capital. The governor and other high-ups were gone by the time Yankees marched in." Caleb wrote of the burning of the depot, the hotel. The looting of stores. "Even ransacked the library, tossed a passel of documents & books out into the muddy street." And there was the white lady who chased two soldiers from her establishment with a shotgun. "You dirty thieves!" she screamed. "You dirty thieves!"

More Yankees were running amok. It worried Caleb. He understood that Sherman planned for his men to live off the land. He understood wrecking railroads and whatever else could be used against Union troops. He understood that along the way Yankees had need of fresh horses and mules. But the senseless destruction, the heedless, needless stealing— with some even robbing colored folks of their few possessions. Caleb feared that some Yankees would get more reckless with his people. General Reb wasn't the only one who grumbled about the thousands of coloreds on the march.

The thought of General Reb called up Caleb's rage. Beyond dangerous, the man was evil. How many minds had he poisoned with his "useless negro" decree? A lot of hogwash that was. Soldiers had more food than they could eat. Private Sykes had told Caleb that meals on the march were better than what could be made of regular army rations. And what harm did it do to let folks ride in a wagon or on a mule?

Night and day, from the way Captain Galloway saw things. "They have more than paid for any clothing, food, and whatnot that comes their way." That was his position when Caleb collected things his people needed.

Back to his diary.

"Capt. G. spoke with Col. L. about the rampages. Was told to think of it as letting off steam. The most Capt. G. can do is ride with foragers & set an example for the likes of Pvts. S. and D."

Caleb put his pencil down. His zeal to make a record of the march had suddenly petered out. But not his thoughts about Mariah.

"Met a young woman today. She came away with us down below Sandersville. Her name is Mariah. She is—"

The march was no place for feelings. Too much danger. Better he put down the diary and pick up the Bible, read from Lamentations or another book with a lot of destruction, affliction, plagues, and the like. The book of Job with that poor man's boils head to toe and ten lifetimes of sorrows—that story would definitely take Caleb's mind off Mariah.

Before Caleb closed his diary, he ended the entry as he always did. With location.

"Camped at Davisboro."

Spilling Memories

Many roads were sandy, hard on the feet.

They slogged through swampland with towering cypress trees veiled in ghostly Spanish moss. Mariah almost lost her footing when she saw a silver-gray crane staring at her as if privy to some great mystery.

Now and then they heard rifles firing or cannon booming in the distance. Just as unnerving were the pillars of smoke. And there'd been that long halt yesterday after a handful of miles thanks to Rebel devilment—bridge at Black Rock Creek burned. Nearly nightfall by the time the laying down of a pontoon bridge was complete and they finally marched on into Louisville. And it already in flames.

But none of it dampened Mariah's spirits. Struggle in freedom was nothing like struggle in slavery. Before she struggled to stay alive and in her right mind. Now the struggles of the march were hitched to striving for a new life.

And last night had a sweet ending. When Caleb came to their campsite with socks, waistcoats, shirts, bandanas, clothespins, tin canteens, bacon, and other random things—and a small wagon—he came early enough to sup with them. Then this morning he came with good news.

"Division won't march today," Caleb told them before he headed out with a forage squad.

"Why?" Mariah had asked. "Some trouble?"

Caleb shook his head. "Soldiers deserve a rest is what I heard."

As the day wore on Mariah saw soldiers do more of what they usually did during a long halt. Fill canteens. Nap. Get up games of chuck-a-luck or whiskey poker. She also saw her people chopping wood for Yankees, currying their horses, blacking their boots.

"Useless negroes." Nobody wanted to be seen as that.

Mariah made herself useful for a while in a mess tent with Zoe, chopping, dicing, slicing for a big batch of Hunger Stew. Mariah also took charge of the coffee, lard, and salt soldiers chipped in as thanks, along with the bucket of liver, chitlins, kidneys, shanks, and bones the regimental butcher let them have.

Later Mariah worked alongside Chloe. She turned bedsheets into bandages, prepared a poultice, and boiled cow feet for a compress. She and Chloe got sugar, a penny or two, sometimes a dime, depending on a soldier's rank, for treating snakebites, sores, or sprains, and for balms to treat blistered feet.

"Ointment and aid!" Chloe called out as she walked among

the soldiers during long halts and on this stay-put day. Mariah walked behind her. Over one shoulder was a beat-up saddlebag with scissors, needles, lance, boiled rags, and gauze. Over the other a sack with bundles of herbs and blended teas, like red oak for stomach miseries and boneset for fevers and other things. As she looked out over the sea of soldiers, Mariah knew that after dark some young women would make themselves useful to Yankees in other ways.

"It ain't so bad," said a slender, doe-eyed girl Mariah figured to be her age.

It was going on dusk. Mariah was riverside, wringing out a pair of socks.

Hagar and a couple of other women had sucked their teeth, snatched up their clothes, and huffed off up the bank when the girl came near.

"You not gonna flounce off like them witches?" asked the girl.

Mariah glanced up. The girl had her mouth poked out, her hands on her hips. "Beg pardon?" Mariah dropped the socks into her basket.

"Ain't you gon' flee too?"

She looked now, not at the girl but at the dirty petticoat over her shoulder. "I got no cause to flee," Mariah said drily. She lifted a pair of britches from the water, reached for a stone slightly larger than her hand.

"Not ashamed to be seen with a fancy girl?"

Mariah commenced scrubbing Zeke's britches. "Happy girl, sad girl, fancy girl," she said without looking up. "It's nothin' to me what kind of girl you are." She rinsed the britches, started wringing them out.

The girl stepped closer to the water's edge, dunked her petticoat. "Name's Praline."

"Mariah."

She got an earful about Praline's life back in Louisville. Like Mariah, mostly Big House labor. Only Praline's white-folks had five young children. "Little hellions. Their mama an idiot. And Master, he—"

One of the huffed-off women cried out. Mariah looked up the bank and saw her sloshing into the river with a long stick to recover a piece of her washing the current sent adrift.

"Anyhow," Praline continued, "when Master John used to hand me around to his men friends, I didn't get nothin' but sore."

By now Mariah was washing a head wrap.

"But these Yanks," Praline continued, "one give me a tent all to myself. Nother a little bottle of scent. It ain't so bad."

With washing done, supper done, Praline, thank goodness, nowhere in sight, and Zeke and Dulcina tucked in, Mariah again found a clear patch not far from the others, again went to herself. Third night of freedom. Third night and still in the dark about the somewhere place. And sad that Caleb hadn't supped with them. Hadn't come after supper either. Mariah tried not to worry.

By now she knew not all foragers came back whistling happy tunes and with plenty of plunder. Hagar had heard of one getting a back full of buckshot and of another found in a ditch, throat cut ear to ear. If Rebels did that to Sherman's soldiers, Mariah knew they'd do worse to a colored man.

"Mind some company?"

Mariah almost jumped out of her skin. So lost in thought, she hadn't heard his footsteps. "Not at all."

What a relief. Caleb had gotten back in one piece.

Mariah fumbled for something else to say as he joined her on the ground. "You took supper with Captain Galloway?"

"Ate on the run. Was helping out at the forge. Shoeing horses, repairing some limber chests."

Mariah couldn't think of anything else to say. Or ask.

Caleb got a small fire going.

As the minutes went by Mariah still couldn't think of anything to say, kept hoping Caleb would come up with conversation. When he didn't she wondered why he came to be with her if he didn't—

Caleb gently tapped the burn scar on her neck.

She flinched.

"What happened here?"

There was a breeze, bearing the scent of pine.

Mariah pursed her lips, looked up at the sky. "Miss Callie

and the tip of a hot poker . . . candle wax on the parlor carpet. I was nearest to blame."

Next, Caleb's finger swept gently across the tiny gash above her left eyebrow.

"Judge Chaney backhanded me. Wore a locket ring on the hand he used."

Another question, then another—before Mariah knew it, she was spilling a host of pent-up memories. The slaps, the kicks, the pinpricks. Then she told him about her pa.

She never knew what her pa did to get the dungeon: a hole in the ground big enough for a body to fit sitting up but too small for a body to move. A piece of board weighed down by a stone covered the pit. A few crude holes allowed just enough air to live.

The man was stuck in the dungeon for one day, two days. At eventide on day three, the dungeon cover, stone and all, blew off in a hurricane rain.

Mariah saw her ma, Patience, fly to the Big House. "Master Chaney, he'll drown!" she screamed. "Master Chaney, please, have mercy!"

Little Mariah grabbed a kettle from their hearth, raced to the dungeon, bailed out water as fast as she could, soon sopping wet herself as she tried to save her pa—and he tried to be heard above the storm's roar.

"No, daughter, git inside 'fore you catch sick. Daughter, git inside."

She kept on with the kettle despite the pain in her thin arms, despite the hard, heavy rain beating her down.

"Love you, daughter," her pa panted, the water at his chin.

Behind a blind of tears, Mariah bailed and bailed and bailed—until Nero descended upon her, snatched the kettle from her hands, dragged her away.

"No!" she screamed, trying in vain to kick and bite free of the hazel-eyed beast. "No!"

Years later Mariah overheard Mordecai tell Esther about that night. "For all of Patience's pleading, Judge Chaney just grunted, 'He be all right,' then knocked back another whiskey."

When done telling Caleb about her pa, it dawned on Mariah that this was the first time she'd ever told anybody about it, the first time she recalled it out loud. Never had a need to. Everybody on the Chaney place knew. The Doubles knew. Others miles around knew. There had never been anybody new to tell. And hardly anybody went in for recollecting nightmares out loud. Or asking. Comfort mostly came in code. A basket of ginger cakes, the soft-singing of "There Is a Balm in Gilead," or whispering "God's watchin'."

For the first time in her life Mariah knew the benefit, the balm of not keeping blistering memories padlocked in her mind.

She wiped her eyes with her sleeve, took a deep breath, managed a half smile.

Caleb handed her a handkerchief. "Didn't mean to cause distress. I don't know what came over me. I just—"

"You caused no distress. Did me a favor. Been a long time since I had a good cry."

"Would you rather be left alone now?"

"No, no." She looked into his eyes. "Stay."

Caleb reached into his coat pocket, brought out a paper packet, and handed it to her.

"What's this?"

"Rock candy."

Mariah undid the packet, popped a few blue crystals into her mouth. "From Captain Galloway?"

Caleb nodded. "I've never known a grown man with such a love for candy."

They burst out laughing. When they settled down into another silence, Mariah longed to tell Caleb more, longed for more relief. She told him about her ma.

About a month after her pa died in the dungeon, Judge Chaney gave up the ghost. Cause of death was a mystery. Miss Callie, bedeviled by the notion that Patience had put a hex on him, ordered Nero to give her fifty lashes.

"Please, Miss Callie, please have mercy!" Mariah threw herself at the woman's feet. They were behind the Big House. Callie Chaney, head to toe in black, beginning with a veil.

"Please, Miss Callie, please don't whip my mama!"

Mariah watched in horror as Nero stripped her mother naked to just below her big belly, tied her up to a rough red oak.

"She ain't put no hex on him!" Mariah clamped her hands over her ears, muffling her mother's screams after Nero laid on the first lash.

"Please! Please!" Mariah sobbed. "I beg you, Miss Callie!"

Nero, in a sweat and grunting, cracked that bullwhip again, again, again.

"My mama believe in Jesus, only in Jesus! She ain't no conjure woman! Please, Miss Callie!"

The whipping continued as did a woman's screams, a little girl's pleas.

At lash thirty-three, Mariah saw Callie Chaney raise a hand, signaling Nero to stop. Mariah, a trembling mass of snot and tears, kissed the woman's feet. "Thank you, ma'am," she whispered.

Miss Callie looked down on her. Voice candy-coated, she said, "She'll get fifty on top of fifty if you don't hush up that hollerin'."

Mariah clamped her hands over her mouth.

Callie Chaney lowered her hand.

Nero resumed his bullwhipping work.

In spilling that memory Mariah also told Caleb about her ma's piercing cries when, after the scourging, Nero doused her back with brine, about how with Josie's help she got her ma to their cabin. But Mariah couldn't bring herself to tell Caleb how she covered her mother's nakedness with her apron, how her stomach churned, how she gagged at the sight of the bloody, shredded back. But she did tell him how Josie ran to Miss Callie, begged her to let Jonah go get Miss Chloe because the baby was coming.

How it seemed a lifetime before Miss Chloe came.

"Then came my mama's last breath, glassy eyes. All I felt was . . . hollow. Too hollow to shed another tear. Life seemed a sorrow without end. I think that day was the last time I cried. Five years ago."

Caleb rubbed her shoulder.

Mariah tensed up, then quickly relaxed. Caleb's hand felt good. "When I finally looked around me, that's when I first laid eyes on the baby boy Miss Chloe was swaddlin'." Mariah took a deep breath. "She said it was for me to name him, so I did. Ezekiel, after our pa."

Mariah heard twigs snap, footsteps.

Jonah. "Everything okay?"

Mariah looked up, saw Jonah standing a few feet away. The fire flickered, flared up, casting long shadows on the pine trees towering above their heads.

SECESH

"Tues., Nov. 29th, 1864."

Caleb paused, stuck on Mariah's story. Such cruelty, brutality was hardly news to him, hardly shocking, but it ate at him in a way that no other story had. Hatred was trying to claim him again.

Best not to dwell on it. Best to focus on the fact that she came through it all sound, didn't wind up like Dulcina. For his own soul's sake, Caleb needed to change the subject.

"Col. L. and his entire staff are stinking drunk, after making 'war' on a distillery," he wrote.

The candle went out. Caleb reached for his brass match safe. With the candle flickering again, he went back and forth on what to write next.

He thought about the waves of people who poured into the march mile after mile. "They come with hopeful hearts.

Every evening somebody brings roasted groundnuts, persimmons, or some other gift to Capt. G.'s tent."

Caleb remembered the bright-looking young men who approached Captain Galloway yesterday. They stood at attention, gave the sharpest salutes. They wanted to join the army.

"Want to help you lick the Rebels!" said one.

Another: "Do our part for freedom!"

Caleb could still see their downcast faces when the captain explained that there were no colored soldiers in Sherman's army. "It's outright lunatic that Sherman won't let hale & hearty colored men join the ranks, but he will only take our labor. To his credit, at least he pays us."

Caleb sharpened his pencil.

"When out foraging today Pvt. D. asked, 'What is secesh?'" In talking with some colored people he got lost every time they spoke of 'secesh.' I explained that it meant Rebel, that it came from 'secessionist.' I then had to explain 'secessionist.' Capt. G. has gotten him and Pvt. S. to give up those beards & use shaving kits every day. He told me this a.m. that they have sworn off cards."

Caleb's mind meandered to Mariah, to how it took every ounce of self-control not to take her in his arms as she talked about what happened to her pa, her ma. How he wished that he could hold her now.

"Camped near Bostwick."

BEHOLD A PALE HORSE

He came out of nowhere like a hound from hell. Mariah was about twenty yards from her campsite, lugging two buckets of water, when he charged toward her.

"You!"

She froze, turned. "Yes, sir?"

Astride a pale horse, he looked Mariah up and down, pointed at his horse. "Water."

Trying not to tremble, she set a bucket before the horse, watched it dip its head down, looked away when it slobbered. Raising her head slightly, she saw the man looking out over the colored section of the camp. Everybody had stopped what they were doing. Mariah saw Chloe hugging Zeke and Dulcina to her bosom. She saw Zoe, Mordecai, and Jonah shrink back into the woods.

"Girl!" the white man barked.

Mariah swallowed. "Yes, sir?"

"Look at me, girl!"

Mariah obeyed but kept her head to the side.

The man was a winter wind, his gaze chilling her to the bone. Spittle in his beard. Face unworldly white. Heavy-lidded blue eyes. Steel blue. Icy. Caleb was right. Deadly.

General Reb.

"Remove the bucket!" he commanded.

Mariah obeyed, holding her breath as he spurred his horse, charged off, then cantered up and down knots of cringing colored people. All eyes lowered as he passed by. A time or two he stopped before a group. His horse reared up, grunted, squealed.

And behold a pale horse! streaked through Mariah's mind, taking her back to that jackleg preacher, Archibald Dyuvil, who came to the Chaney place at Christmastime. The man always took his text from the Book of Revelation, had a hard fascination with the Four Horsemen of the Apocalypse. The word "apocalypse" terrified little Mariah. More so after she asked her pa what it meant.

"End of days."

Mariah could see, could hear that preacher reading one passage again and again. About the opening of seals, the noise of thunder, and four beasts saying, "Come and see . . . Come and see . . . Come and see . . ."

A white horse, a red horse, a black horse—then the preacher paused. Rising to his full height, he bellowed, "And I looked, and behold a pale horse and his name that sat on him was Death, and Hell followed with him."

Bible slammed shut, he shouted, "The Four Horsemen of the Apocalypse be War, Famine, Disease, and Death!"

While General Reb taunted her people, Mariah remained motionless. She didn't move a muscle until a trail of dust was all that remained of the pale horse and its pale-eyed rider.

The man left evil in the air and Mariah sick to her stomach. A cup of red cedar bark tea didn't help much.

"Did he hurt anybody?" asked Caleb later that evening.

"No," replied Mariah. "Just seemed out to terrify."

"But thank the Lord, we had wagons hid like you told us," said Chloe. "Nobody had to scatter and scramble."

Mariah wished Caleb didn't have to go to the forge, wished he could stay longer than the time it took for him to hand out goods.

And behold a pale horse! Those words haunted Mariah as she lay in the tent later that night, praying for sleep, for General Reb's face to be wiped from memory. No sooner than it began to fade her mind was flooded with frightening news on the day's grapevine. Rachel had heard of soldiers in another part of the march finding colored people tiresome. "Cast them out from their camp. Cast them out without so much as a kernel of corn. Sent them to their death or to a maulin' for sure when Rebels come upon those poor souls."

Hagar had heard about a man who didn't move fast enough when some soldiers ordered him to groom their horses. "Whipped the fella with their belts to get the name and place of his owner, then hog tied him and hauled him two miles back to the plantation, dumped him at his owner's front door." She had also heard that days back a couple of Yankees had snatched a young girl, dragged her into some woods, and—

Rest easy.

If only Caleb was there to repeat those words himself.

Rest easy.

In slavery Mariah had never known what it was to feel safe. And now she didn't feel safe on the march.

She remembered Caleb's calmness during that first wagon ride. How sure he was of things. Mariah fixed her mind on that to banish the storm clouds in her mind.

MANY THOUSAND GONE

Caleb had pulled a muscle in his back in the forge the night before. Captain Galloway spared him forage duty. "Rest up. Heal quick," he said.

Caleb was sure he would with the comfrey poultice Chloe was applying to his back. As he sat there on a carbine crate, he saw his injury as a blessing in disguise. It meant a whole day with Mariah, who looked like a new penny.

With the poultice in place and his back bound, Caleb harnessed and hitched the horses.

"I'll load," said Mariah.

"Let me help with some things."

"I insist."

Caleb didn't argue. He stepped over to the cook spot for another cup of coffee. He was impressed with the orderly way Mariah got Dulcina and Zeke in the wagon, then the provisions and belongings.

Things were a little more chaotic with the wagon Morde-cai was set to drive carrying Hagar, Hosea, Rachel, Miriam, the Doubles.

Ben placed little Rose on his pony.

"Where's Jonah?" Caleb asked.

"Captain Galloway asked him last night to report early to run messages," replied Mariah.

Another blessing, thought Caleb.

Then a shock.

Wagon loaded, Mariah was climbing into the driver's seat.

Caleb poured the rest of his coffee onto the ground.

"What do you think you're doing, young lady?" He had reached the wagon.

"What it look like?"

"I ain't crippled."

"But one wrong move and you could go from bad to worse."

"You can truly handle horses?" Caleb teased Mariah. "You sure I can trust you with my life? How I know you won't drive us off a cliff or into a gully?"

"Caleb, you can trust me. With your life. With anything else."

Caleb reached into his back pocket for his buckskin gloves, and handed them to Mariah.

"Who taught you to drive?" They were about a half mile along.

"My pa."

Behind them some distance, people riding on mules, in oxcarts and wagons, along with ones walking had been singing "Didn't My Lord Deliver Daniel." Now they switched to "Many Thousand Gone."

No more auction block for me.
No more, no more.
No more auction block for me . . .

On they sang of terrors, of toil. No more peck of corn, driver's lash, pint of salt, hundred lash, mistress call, children stole.

No more slavery chains for me.

The refrain was a shout.

Many thousand gone!

"Yes, thank God." Mariah sighed. "Thank God, many thousand gone."

"Come on," said Caleb. "Let's hear you sing."

"Oh no, you don't want that."

"I bet you're a regular little songbird. Bet you have a lovely voice."

Mariah looked at him out of the corner of her eye. "Caleb, I can't carry a tune to save my life."

He had never met a girl so guileless. It made her all the more adorable. "What else did your pa teach you?"

"Swim, fish, trap."

Mariah's hands were practically swimming in his gloves, but the girl was more than making do. Caleb had to admit it. Mariah could drive. Right amount of give and take on the reins. Knew how to take a curve. Not once did she crack the whip.

Caleb found it hard to keep his eyes on the road or on anything else other than Mariah. He was trying to occupy his mind with the silky, swirling bands of clouds when Mariah asked, "When you go out with a forage team, do you bust into homes and stores like we heard soldiers do?"

"I stay clear of all that. Just load what I'm told to load."

"So how is it that you're able to bring us things? Seen you give things to Hagar and others too."

"On occasion I find things lying in the street, on the side of a road. Banjo, jackets, hats, parasols, trousers. Cases where soldiers weren't in a mood to take, just ransack. Something in particular you need?"

"No. Just curious."

"Other times I put it out there some of the things people could use. Pay for it with favors. Shoe a horse and things like that, or trade with something a soldier asked me to be on the lookout for."

"That's how you got my boots. Put it out that there was a need?"

"Uh-huh. Lately, most of what I come by is thanks to Privates Sykes and Dolan. They keep an eye out. Oftentimes soldiers just grab and dash. Don't really know what they got till they camp and start sorting."

"The first time those two handed out food they looked at us like . . . creatures from the moon."

Caleb laughed. "Most of them have no idea, no custom with being person to person, white with colored. But Private Sykes and Private Dolan they are trying. One of the blacksmiths with the Fourteenth is an uncle of Private Sykes. So I help the uncle out at his forge sometimes. And Sykes helps me out."

"Blacksmith, that's your trade?"

"Uh-huh."

"Trained up from young?"

"Yup."

Caleb felt uneasy about this turn in the conversation. He was fast thinking about how he could turn it back to the march.

"Can I ask you something, Caleb?"

"Go ahead."

"Your speech has a—you talk with a little more polish than I've ever heard from colored. Did your master let you learn openly?"

Caleb looked away, rubbed his chin. "I guess you could say I was allowed to learn openly."

"So your whitefolks wasn't all-out crazy?"

Caleb shrugged.

"Your ma and pa, they were on the same place?"

Caleb started to tell her the truth, then thought better of it. Now wasn't the right time. He just wanted to enjoy her. "Yeah, my folks they lived together," he finally said.

"Were they—"

Thank goodness—a bugle call came. *Halt!*

As soon as Mariah brought the horses to a stop, Caleb eased down from the wagon. "Want to find out why he stopped. Won't be long."

"Another bridge Rebels burned," Caleb explained when he returned.

"Any idea how long before the pion—I mean, the pontoniers be finished?"

Caleb smiled. What a head she was developing for all this soldier business in just a few days. "Not long," he replied. And now that the conversation had moved from him to the march, Caleb was determined to keep it that way.

"They say Rebels in all kinds of confusion. Can't make out if Uncle Billy's boys are aiming for Macon or Augusta. Some predict he will cut east and storm South Carolina."

"Wait now, who's Uncle Billy?"

"General Sherman. Troops call him Uncle Billy," Caleb explained. "Loyal to the death. Anyhow, soldiers sent on destruction raids are going above and beyond. When wrecking railroad track, bending rails into hairpins and neckties not enough for some. They aim for something more insulting to Southern soil, like twisting rails into a giant US."

"Us?"

"No, short for United States."

"Why all the destruction? Why don't Sherman simply hunt down as many Rebel soldiers as he can?"

"Rebel soldiers not his main concern."

"Who is?"

"Sherman's out to terrify civilians—the everyday people. Figures if he makes their lives hell, they'll clamor for Georgia to quit the Confederacy. Surrender."

Mariah looked worried. "But what if it don't work, what if—?"

"With or without Georgia, Confederacy is on its last legs. Lost cause."

Mariah didn't look like she believed him. She had gone from the picture of delight to the picture of worry.

"Really?" she asked.

"Last summer, in July, y'all heard about Gettysburg and Vicksburg?"

"The battles?"

Caleb nodded. "Gettysburg made Rebels abandon hope of invading the North. After Vicksburg the Union was on the way to getting back control of the Mississippi." Caleb saw Mariah still looked worried. "And by smashing up Atlanta, Sherman destroyed a chief source of weapons and other supplies."

"Caleb, couldn't there be some battle up ahead that the Union could lose?"

"Could be, but the Union will win the war."

"But what if they don't? What if—if the Union lose . . . will the Captain Galloways of the world have to—"

Now Mariah looked downright terrified.

"Have to do what?"

"Give us back?"

"No one's giving you back, Mariah. Nobody's giving anybody back."

Ten minutes later, they were on the move again. When they reached a wide stretch Caleb saw Mordecai's wagon gaining on them.

"Mordecai and Chloe?" Caleb asked. "I notice most nights he cozies to her the most. Was there a time when they were, you know—"

"Coupled up?"

"Uh-huh."

Mariah shook her head. "Looks to me like Mordecai out to make up for lost time."

"Lost time?"

"Yep." Mariah turned to Caleb. "I reckon about . . . thirty years."

Caleb asked God to let him grow old with Mariah.

"The way I heard it, they had eyes for each other, but as a

boy Mordecai vowed to never marry so long as he was in bond-age. Didn't want to ever see his wife or children abused."

"That's some sacrifice—and Chloe strikes me as one of the finest women God ever made."

"A saint."

Caleb noticed that Mariah was squinting. He removed his hat, plopped it on her head, and tipped the brim down.

"Thanks much." She smiled. "Anyhow, Miss Chloe, she tried to get Mordecai to budge by tellin' him that her white-folks wasn't all-out vicious. And that was true. Never struck any of their slaves. Never had anybody whipped. Never had that many slaves to begin with. I think five at most. The Doubles, their butler, Jim, who died last year, and the house-keeper, Gertie, who decided to stay. But back to Miss Chloe. See, she argued that if her whitefolks ever gave her a cussin', he would not be there to hear it. She said them bein' on two different places was good. Would make their Sundays together much sweeter."

"Thirty years, that's a long time to hold out on love. Think they'll marry now?"

"I hope so. They long overdue for some happiness."

In a different time and place Caleb would have inched closer and slipped his arm around Mariah's waist.

"If you don't mind me asking, you and Jonah. You two ever—?"

"No."

Caleb loved the quick response. So definite.

"Jonah's another brother to me. Nothing more."

"Seems to me Jonah would like to be more than a brother."

Mariah pursed her lips. "Can we talk about somethin' else?"

Caleb gave her a salute. "Yes, Captain Mariah!"

"Captain?" she said. "Can't I be your general?"

Caleb melted under Mariah's sly and frisky smile.

Sweetest day of my life, Caleb thought later that night, a night bearing easy breezes and calm. Just about everybody seemed in a light mood.

Hosea on the banjo he'd found for him. Ben playing the spoons. One gaggle of youngsters did the cakewalk. Another was patting juba.

Jonah was the exception. Sour all through supper and afterward he stomped off. Caleb was glad he did. But he hoped Jonah would cool off, recognize that he wasn't the one at fault. A man can't keep what he never had.

Caleb was grateful to Mordecai and the Doubles for once again giving him and Mariah private time. After supper, with oversight of Dulcina, they passed the time with Hosea and Hagar's band.

Caleb didn't mind sharing Mariah with Zeke at all. He enjoyed watching her tickle him, make funny faces.

When Mariah settled Zeke down and began darning a sock, Caleb went to work on the timberdoodle he'd started the other day. As she talked, Caleb whittled away.

"Cabbages big as moons!" Mariah exclaimed, recalling her ma's garden.

When she fell silent, Caleb feared bad memories were creeping up. But then she jumped up, smiled. "I want to show you some things."

She returned with a pouch. In it, a tin. In the tin, wrapped in a handkerchief, twelve blue glass beads. "Was a Christmas gift from Pa to Ma. Wore them in her hair most Sundays."

"She must have looked lovely." Caleb imagined Mariah on a sunny Sunday with blue glass beads in her hair.

Caleb's conscience took him to task for sharing so little about himself, as Mariah recalled her pa making her ma a new spinning wheel, taking delight in carving tiny flowers on the whorl.

And there was the cedar trunk he made. And a fiddle for her one Christmas. "Like his, only smaller, made of a gourd and groundhog hide. Bow from bamboo and horsehair."

"And I'm guessing your pa taught you to play."

Mariah nodded. "His fiddle was his peace at the end of a day. Not much for fast tunes. Windin' down kind mostly."

"You still got your fiddle?"

Mariah shook her head. "Wore that thing out." From the pouch she brought out a chisel and a small wooden mallet. "These my main keepsakes of my pa." From her apron pocket she brought out the jackknife. "This was his too."

"Whoa!" Caleb laughed. "I'll be sure not to rile you. You could do some real harm with that thing."

Mariah looked on edge.

"What, did I hit a nerve, Mariah?" he asked, looking down at the bone-handled knife in her hand. A six-inch blade, he reckoned. "Mariah, tell me you've only had to use that knife for cutting twine, bark, and such."

"Yeah, twine, bark, and such." She smiled.

Caleb didn't believe her. It was a put-on smile, but he wasn't going to push it.

Caleb was almost finished with the timberdoodle's long, needle-thin beak when Mariah told him about times her pa blacked out the windows, brought out a speller from beneath a floorboard in the back of their cabin, then had her and her ma gather around the hearth.

Caleb handed Zeke the timberdoodle.

"My bird?"

"Yes, your bird, my boy," replied Caleb with a tug on Zeke's cap.

"That's precious," said Mariah.

You're precious, thought Caleb.

"Thanky," said Zeke.

"Most welcome," said Caleb.

As Mariah delighted in Zeke zigging and zagging his timberdoodle, Caleb imagined her lips upon his, his hand—

Once again her joy was gone. Her eyes were no longer on her brother, but on something—or someone—behind him.

Caleb turned around. In the distance stood Jonah gawping, looking vexed.

Goodness Like Mint

Onward Mariah marched to the somewhere place, feeling the strain by day six. A little more jittery when a bobcat yowled or cannon boomed. A little more anguished by scenes along the way bringing to mind the end of days.

Chimneys the only things left standing in some towns.

The stench from the burning—homes, buildings, gin houses, bales of cotton.

Pillars of smoke, pillars of fire.

Women wailing, children's hoarse cries. But silent as the grave was the white girl Mariah spotted spearing a pocket gopher on this day.

Stringy blond hair. Stick-skinny legs a mass of scabs and bruises. Bruises on her face, neck. And welts. The girl's dress, crusty-looking and tattered, was a burlap sack and never bleached. "Flour" was stamped across the girl's back. She moved like it hurt to walk.

The girl picked up the gopher, put it behind her back as they passed by. Mariah gave her a slight smile.

"What you lookin' at, you filthy nigra?"

Mariah felt pity more than anything else. If goodness was like mint . . . She sighed, thinking of a bright March day long ago and making a mental note to tell Caleb about it when she saw him that evening.

"Whatcha gon' do with all them stones?" she asked her ma.

They were behind their cabin. Mariah dangled on the post and plank fence around their patch. All winter they'd been feeding it ashes, eggshells, bones, fish heads, other scraps. Now planting time was on the horizon. Her ma had already turned the soil. Her pa had just brought over a wheelbarrow full of stones.

"Stones are for the mint," Patience explained. "Putting in mint this year."

"But can't nothin' grow in stones," Mariah puzzled, crinkling her nose.

Patience beckoned her over, pointed to the back corner of the garden patch, told her that's where the mint would live. "It'll spread if it ain't hedged," her ma explained, then told her how mint roots roam under the soil and send up shoots inches, feet away, making more roots, and those roots then roam, send up shoots, making new roots. "And up comes more mint. If I don't wall it off, mint will take over the garden. We'll wind up with no corn and cabbages, no beans and tomatoes, no peppers, no goosefoot, no squash, no okra."

Mariah asked if the mint could spread all the way out to Riddleville Road if there were no stones in its way.

"Possible," said Patience.

"Could the roots roam and shoot up, roam and shoot up, over all of Georgia—over the whole Southland?"

"Wouldn't that be a sight!" Patience replied. "And just imagine what a fine world this would be if goodness was like mint."

"And nobody troubled it with stones."

Her ma's mint left Mariah's mind during a halt before a row of dilapidated double-pen cabins. Two boys, one cream, one caramel, stood in the door of one. Big heads. Large, empty eyes. Matted hair. Spindly. No shoes. One, about Zeke's age, was sucking his thumb.

Mariah waved. "Come on!" she called out. "Tell your people to come on! Come to freedom!" She was about to fetch the boys when a rheumy-eyed, rickety man, bent almost in two, came to the door. "Git inside!" he growled. After the little boys obeyed, the old man shut the door.

What would keep that old man from taking freedom? Too broke-down to care anymore? Was he like Josie? Staying because someone he loved got hired out? His son? Was he the little boys' pa? Where was their ma?

Josie, baby Sarah, Little Jack. How were they faring? Had Nero taken off? If he didn't, Mariah hoped he got the hire-out and was put to hard labor building barricades, digging trenches, and whatever else Rebels needed doing to free up a white man to fight. Serve Nero right. Mordecai had told Mariah that hire-outs died like flies, something they kept from Josie. If Nero didn't take off and didn't get hired out, Mariah prayed to God he wasn't giving Josie torment.

Of all the men to be on guard against—pattyrollers, Judge Chaney's brother with his thick, fleshy fingers, tarrying a fortnight most times, Master Robert—Nero was the worst.

First time was in the barn when she was milking a cow. Nero crept up behind her, mumbled something about her growing so pretty, laid a hand on her back. "You mine," he slurred.

All on fire, Mariah grabbed an empty pail, swung it with all her might, left Nero clutching his side when she fled.

Weeks later Nero tried to shove her into the corncrib. By then Mariah went nowhere without her jackknife. She whipped it out in time to ward off Nero.

"Second time you refuse me," Nero had barked. "Ain't gon' give you but so many chances. Six, thas all. You don't be mine six time I come for you, I will tell Miss Callie you due a whippin'."

Along with Miss Callie's madness, Mariah had to deal with Nero's cat-and-mouse.

Him looking about to charge on her when she was getting a wash pot going, then steering clear and snickering.

Him peeping at her through the cookhouse door, making nasty gestures.

Him trying to sneak up on her when she headed to the chicken coop.

Him once just staring at her, mumbling about extra dresses, more food, and how she was to respect the white in him.

Her shoving the cedar trunk against her cabin door. Nightly.

The day before Yankees descended on the Chaney place, Nero had preyed on Mariah for the sixth time. In the barn again. She didn't use a pail to fend him off this time or her jackknife. She used her knee.

"Yo' time up!" Nero raged, clutching his groin. "You fool heifer, yo' time up!"

Mariah knew the only reason she didn't get whipped was because, what with all the commotion coming from Sandersville, Callie Chaney kept Jonah and Nero busy hiding silver and other valuables.

More than once Mariah was tempted to tell Jonah about Nero's dirty ways—tempted to even turn it into a tale of all-out outrage. She knew Jonah would hurt Nero, maybe even—

She couldn't. Couldn't set Jonah up for hard trouble. Hitting a slave driver was second to hitting a white man. If Jonah hurt or even killed Nero, he could be made to suffer a hundred different ways.

Just as Mariah prayed that no outlaws came to the Chaney place, so she prayed that Nero had gone away. She chided herself for not trying harder to talk Josie out of staying. But then she remembered Josie's resolve, reminded herself that she could no more have talked Josie out of staying than Josie could have talked her out of leaving.

Mariah had to leave, doubly so for Zeke's sake. Her brother would never be strapping-strong like Jonah. With the way Zeke's mind came and went, there'd be a limit to the work that he could do. The older he got, the harder Callie Chaney would be on him. Maybe even label him useless.

No more. That worry was behind her now. All the wickedness too. That thought alone helped Mariah soldier on.

No more, she reminded herself as her feet burned, stomach griped, temples throbbed.

No more, she thought when a wagon wheel got stuck in a rut and she had to help with the unloading, the pushing, the lifting, the loading up again.

No more, Mariah thought when reminding herself that it was only right that she and Miriam walk the most. And now Ben. His pony died during the night.

On this day, like other days, Dulcina and Zeke always rode in the wagon. Mariah learned early on that if on two feet Zeke was apt to stop and spin, Dulcina to wander off, like she sometimes did when they camped. Just last night, Mariah heard stirring in the tent, then saw Dulcina poking her head through the flaps. As Mariah got her settled back down, she saw the strangest look in her eyes. Delight.

"Texas." Meowed, caterwauled, whispered—that was still the only word Dulcina uttered. But now Dulcina sometimes fell into lapses of silent talking. No sound, only lips moving. Mariah feared things were getting worse, feared there was nothing she or others could do except keep close watch.

Dulcina was beyond repair, Mariah had concluded, but she held out hope for Zeke, growing more curious by the day—sometimes by the hour.

"Big worm have feet?" He pointed at a red-black-yellow-ringed creature slithering at the base of a tree.

"Ma, when you gon' learn me to fly?" Mariah followed his gaze. She shared in his delight at the sight of a bluebird on the wing.

Though feeling poorly, with the brutal sun helping none, Mariah wanted her brother to keep asking questions.

Of the red-black-yellow-ringed slithering thing, "No, Zeke, it don't have feet and it ain't a worm. It's a king snake."

"Keen snake."

"King snake," she repeated. "And as some snakes do awful harm, you steer clear of all. You hear me?"

Zeke nodded rapidly as Mariah had done years ago. It was during one of what her pa called their Sunday "excursions."

If they set out for the river, her pa didn't just help her perfect how to bait, how to wait, when to slack. He also had a lesson on something else, like how to tell sweet from brackish water.

Fond memories flowed of her pa teaching her how to trap a possum versus rabbit.

Names of trees—hawthorne, spruce, buckeye, sweet gum.

How to tell a deer's disposition by the bleat.

And birds—coot, grackle, meadowlark, mourning dove, timberdoodle, bobwhite, quail—Mariah's pa taught her their names and had her listen closely to their songs.

"Learn all you can," he always said. "Never know what will come in handy."

Just as he had given her the gift of curiosity, so now on the march Mariah encouraged the same in her little brother— though she had never asked her pa to teach her to fly.

"No, Zeke, I won't be teaching you to fly."

"But . . ."

Mariah saw Zeke strain to string a thought together. "You learned me to swim like fishies," he finally said.

"That's different." Mariah laughed.

"Why?"

"People can swim. People can't fly." She waited for Zeke to ask "Why?" stumped as to how she'd answer.

But she didn't have to. Her brother's mind had moved on, to a chipmunk at the edge of the road. It twitched its nose, reared up on its hind legs, and twitched its nose again. Zeke twitched his nose, then gave the critter a salute.

Watching her brother in his new bliss, Mariah tried to reclaim that joy she felt when she joined the march, tried to get back that feeling that she could run, run, run, not faint. Now . . .

Hazards, hardships—nothing new. But now hourly, daily, the ground beneath her feet was always shifting. Not a minute passed that Mariah wasn't grateful for the journey, but she was tired of the march.

Tired of still being trapped.

But the march was her only hope. Couldn't take off and make her way to a place of her choosing, not that she had any place to choose. New York was a fantasy. Milledgeville was the only place she'd ever been. When she learned that they were camped at Louisville or Bostwick—they were just words. Mariah had no idea where she was. And only one certainty: clinging to Yankees was clinging to freedom.

As they neared the campground, Mariah thought about her ma and her mint, Zeke and his peppermint sticks—mostly shards by now. By day the pouch was tied around his rope belt. At night, looped around a wrist. Again and again Mariah urged her brother to eat his sweets. "After a while all you gon' have is a bag of dust."

Again and again Zeke shook his head, then said, "My freedoms!"

Again and again Mariah thought, *If only freedom came with wings.* She wouldn't be on a march to another's somewhere place, but high in the sky soaring on wings like that golden eagle's, scouting out her own somewhere place, a place where goodness grew like mint.

So Beat Down

When Caleb checked in on them that morning Mariah looked so beat down. What a shame after their glorious yesterday together. Fitful sleep, he guessed. When he learned about Ben's pony, he knew that didn't help.

Before he headed out, Caleb made a mental note to be on the lookout for something that might cheer Mariah up. Dress? Straw hat? Cloth for a head wrap? Taffy? Then he remembered that he already had something that would lift her spirits.

Earlier that morning, Captain Galloway showed him on a map the line of march for the next few days. As Caleb studied the route, he had a hunch about the final destination. When the captain revealed that one division, with General Kilpatrick's cavalry, would form a flying column, striking out toward Augusta "to convince Rebels that we are gunning for

Augusta"—Caleb's hunch was even stronger. It was a place he was eager to see, a fine place to make a new beginning. At least it was before the war.

Caleb started doing rough figures in his head. Printing press. Ink. Paper. Printer. Rent. Days ago, when he told Captain Galloway about his dream, he learned the captain had a cousin in the business, knew a thing or two.

Caleb tallied up the figures the captain had given him, thought about the sum he'd left Atlanta with, Sherman's pay. Not bad. The enterprise was doable.

But there was something he forgot to factor in, something that wasn't on his mind when he latched onto his dream. Till now he was the only one in the picture. Figured he could make the shop double as home till he got the business built up. But now he wanted Mariah in the picture. He'd need to do more figuring, taking into account Mariah and Zeke. And when the war ended, he'd probably have to get supplies from the North with so much of the South in wreck and ruin. Everything would be more expensive. "Where there's a will, there's a way," Caleb whispered to himself, when the squad reached a farm. He decided to scratch the printing press and heed Captain Galloway's advice to contract with a printer at the start. That would save him about a thousand dollars.

Seeing Mariah in the picture made Caleb remember the moment in the wagon when he had an urge to tell her about himself. Skirting her questions wasn't far from lying. Caleb felt bad about that.

Caleb, you can trust me. With your life. With anything else.

Of course he wanted to trust her. If he didn't, how could he love her?

Tonight. Tonight will be the night, he decided, as he loaded sacks of rice into his wagon. Tonight he'd tell Mariah his story. If he paired it with news of the likely somewhere place it would all go down easier.

LASHING FURY

Lonesome and pale was the late afternoon moon. Mariah was so grateful to be out from under the broiling sun.

Thankful, too, that Mordecai and Chloe had volunteered to haul water.

The tent. She was strong enough to tackle that after getting Zeke and Dulcina settled. Maybe once she had the tent up she'd crawl inside, grab a quick nap before supper. Just a few winks. Just a little quiet near the end of a day that started off with trouble. And there was more to it than her waking up tired and Ben's tears over his pony.

At daybreak, Hagar had lashed out at Miriam for spilling water on their fire. "You clumsy fool, you!"

Minutes later two other women got into a shouting match over clothespins.

About an hour after Caleb headed out to forage, two men

Mariah only knew by sight got into a shoving match over a can of beans. One pulled out a razor.

"Saddlebag!" Chloe had called out.

Mariah helped Chloe tend to the one got his cheek slashed, while Mordecai talked the other man down.

Mariah was nearly done with the tent when Jonah came over loaded with firewood.

"Need a word," he said.

Mariah looked up, troubled by his tone. "Say on."

"Private."

Jonah put the firewood down, took the mallet from her hand, helped her up. "Miss Zoe?" He nodded at Zeke and Dulcina, then dropped the mallet on the ground.

Zoe, stirring a pot, nodded back.

"You stay put, Zeke," said Mariah.

"Yeah, Ma," replied Zeke, zigzagging his timberdoodle.

Dulcina was crouched beside him, caught up in silent talking. But Mariah didn't worry. Dulcina never wandered off when engaged in that.

Mariah didn't appreciate the tight grip Jonah had on her arm. With his strides so wide, she had to practically skip to keep up.

"Jonah, what's happened?"

He stopped between two live oaks dripping Spanish moss.

Had Jonah found out where the march would end? Did he have news of a battle? But why would he take her aside for that? He'd want the rest to know too.

Jonah looked so betwixt and between. Was he bearing good news or bad?

He shoved his hands into his pockets, paced. "You said in freedom you would . . ."

Mariah smelled ashes in the air. "Would what?"

"Get on with life . . . like men and women do."

She had been dreading this moment, had fretted over what to say. Be direct, no beating around the bush—that's what she had decided. But now, face to face with Jonah, in the clear light of day, Mariah lost her nerve. "We only on the road, Jonah. Don't know how many more miles till we reach a place permanent, a place safe—"

"We been free six days now. And you said in freedom me and you—"

"I said . . . maybe, Jonah. Maybe."

"Wasn't no maybe." Jonah paced again. "I remember how you looked at me, so tender that day, like I matter to you."

"That's not how it was," Mariah snapped, then regretted that. She didn't want to bruise Jonah.

Mariah tempered her tone. "Jonah, you always have, always will matter to me." Now Mariah paced. "And natu-rally I was lookin' at you tender that day. Your ma wasn't in the ground two weeks." She swallowed. "You were all jumbled up inside."

Jonah took Mariah by the shoulders, his touch gentle. "Never been jumbled up when it come to you."

Those had been days of confusion for Mariah too. Even then, when her life was so cramped, so bitter and Jonah so thoughtful . . . She had worried that maybe something was wrong with her. Maybe she was unnatural. After all, Jonah was a good man. Why didn't she love him? But she knew she didn't. And she thought it more unnatural, downright wrong, to take up with a man she did not love.

When her ma told her a day would come when big boys and even men would notice her, Mariah had taken to heart some strong advice.

"Don't let just any man have your grace." Patience was spinning flax. "Mariah, you keep yourself for a good man." Mariah could hear the wheel rattle and whirl, rattle and whirl. "A good man. Like your pa. On top of him being good, he needs to be a true love."

"How to know a true love?"

"When you get beyond the moonstruck stage and you hit a rough patch, but find you can't stay mad at him for long."

Mariah had never been moonstruck over Jonah. But back when his ma passed, she couldn't bring herself to tell him the truth. Then Mordecai's vow came to mind.

"Not until I'm free," she had told Jonah so as not to hurt his feelings. "Not unless I'm free will I take a man or bring a child into this world." When Jonah asked if he would be that man if freedom came, Mariah had said, "Maybe." She hoped Jonah would lose interest, get impatient, go court one of the girls on the Ramsey or Rucker place. Like then, so now, Mariah couldn't tell Jonah the truth.

She wriggled out of his grasp, took a step back, folded her arms across her chest. "Jonah, we not fully free."

"What you mean we ain't fully free?"

"True, we out from under Callie Chaney, but—"

"We free, Mariah, we free!"

"Not fully, Jonah!" Mariah paced again. "The way I see it, the way it sometimes feels, it's like Yankees are our masters now. We wake, eat, march, halt, sleep all on their say. Ever at their mercy." Mariah stopped, looked up at Jonah. "How you know we won't get split up, you sent to be with a different regiment, brigade, or—"

"Captain Galloway won't let that happen."

"Captain Galloway got ones above him."

Jonah shoved his hands back into his pockets. "I feel it in my bones, Mariah, we'll get to full freedom . . . have a . . . have new tomorrows. Won't be beggarly, neither." Jonah stepped toward Mariah. "I looked out for us."

What on earth was he talking about?

"It's what I signaled right before we left the Chaney place. I didn't tell Yanks all where Miss Callie had me hide things."

Jonah smiled wide. "I snuck away some. Small things. Spoons, forks, match safe, little box like a casket, case for her visit cards, one of the judge's flasks, things like that . . . Judge's gold watch. Got that too."

Mariah was shocked. She never expected such cunning from Jonah.

"That ain't all." He reached into his vest pocket, brought out a twenty-dollar gold piece.

"Where'd you get that?"

"From where Miss Callie had me hide it in the henhouse."

Mariah knew the price of some things from being Miss Callie's pack animal during her spur-of-the-moment trips to Milledgeville to visit with kin and spend big at the clothing store, tailor, confectionary, dry goods store, and the shops where she bought liquor and bitters. Mariah knew the price of clocks, tinware, and sundry other items from the peddlers who called at the back door. She imagined the food, the clothes— the land—that one gold coin could buy.

"Got five more like it."

There was something weaselly about the look on Jonah's face. Something unsavory. Like a soldier sidling up to a fancy girl. Mariah took a step back.

"There's things I lack, Mariah. Never learnt to read. Not good with words in speech. But one thing I know, I can take care of you—and Zeke. Was y'all I had my mind on when I took the silver, the gold."

"Mighty sweet of you, Jonah, but—"

From another pocket Jonah brought a gold spray of posies, a diamond at the center of each flower. He held the brooch out to Mariah. "For you."

"I don't want that!" Mariah backed away, remembering the pinpricks.

"What's wrong?"

"I want *nothing* that belonged to that woman."

Jonah pushed his hat back on his head, ran a hand across his brow. He laughed.

Was he mocking her? "What's so funny?"

"You." Jonah put the brooch back into his pocket. "You say you want *nothing* that belong to that woman?"

"Still don't see cause for laughter."

"Mariah, *you* belonged to that woman. *I* belonged to that woman. Your *brother* belonged to that woman."

"Your point?"

"If we don't belong to her no more, then what I carried off don't neither."

Mariah's arms were folded across her chest again. She knew what was coming when Jonah's eyes lingered on her lace-up boots.

"You know what else?" he sneered. "Them boots didn't drop down from heaven. They once belonged to somebody. Somebody like Miss Callie, I reckon, yet you was mighty pleased to—"

"That's different!" Mariah snapped.

"How?"

"They didn't belong to Miss Callie!" Mariah looked away. If only she could make Jonah go away. "And I had need of better shoes."

"Wasn't the gift. Was the giver!" Jonah yelled.

"You sound crazy." For the first time in her life Mariah was afraid of Jonah.

Nostrils flared. His footsteps were heavy as he paced, eyes lashing fury. "I see how you look at him!" Jonah muttered. "Always talkin' to him!"

Mariah turned her back on Jonah, stepped away.

"Look at me, Mariah!"

A few steps on she looked over her shoulder. Jonah was charging.

Mariah spun around. "I *know* you not about to lay a hand on me!" Now she was breathing hard. Now her eyes were lashing fury. "You don't rule me, Jonah! You have no say in how I look at anybody, who I talk to, what I put on my own two feet!"

"No, Mariah, no! Not tryna rule you," Jonah said softly. "It's jus' that you, me, we come up together. Know each other. Have the same story. Caleb's different. He's—"

"Don't start that again!"

"Mark my word, sumpin' ain't right." Jonah snorted. "He hidin' sumpin'. Got an air about him like he had some rule. You ask me, I say Caleb was a driver."

"That's foolishness, Jonah!" Mariah was fit to be tied. And so tired.

Tired of doing her business and helping Zeke do his in the woods.

Tired of the contortions she had to go through to keep herself and him halfway clean.

Tired of the smell of old folks who couldn't help wetting themselves and the folks, young and old, who came down with the flux.

Tired of colicky, mewling babies.

Tired of the stench of burning timber, steel, cotton.

Tired of bracing for cannon boom, rifle fire.

Tired of seeing turkey buzzards circling carcasses of hogs and cattle Yankee butchers left behind.

Tired of worrying about being seen as useless.

And now so tired of Jonah. "All Caleb's done for us day in, day out, and *you* run him down?" Now Mariah was angry enough to tell Jonah the truth. "Jonah, I can't see gettin' on with life like men and women with you. I don't love you, Jonah."

Mariah headed for their campsite. She didn't get far before Jonah caught up with her, grabbed her by the arm.

"Get off me!" Mariah shouted, loud enough for others to hear. She strode on faster. As she did, she saw Mordecai and Chloe rise from an ammunition crate, Zoe shake her head.

She was a few yards away from them when Caleb pulled up to their campsite.

He jumped down from the buckboard. "Mariah, what happened?"

Mariah shook her head. "Nothin'." She sniffled. "Jonah—we just had a—a little mix-up."

Zeke looked up, scrambled over. "Ma cry?" He hugged Mariah around the waist.

Mariah patted her brother's head. "I'm not cryin', Zeke," she cooed.

Zeke handed her his timberdoodle.

"Thank you, Zeke." Mariah gave the bird a halfhearted zigzag, then stopped when she looked up.

Jonah was charging.

And eyeballing Caleb hard.

Driver!

Caleb looked up, too, saw Jonah in a rage, a rage rising with his every heavy step. In a few wide strides, Jonah was within a few feet of him, shaking his hat in his face. "Say what kind you were!"

Caleb took a step back. "Whoa now, Jonah. Don't know what you mean."

Jonah got within a foot of Caleb.

Mordecai stepped in between them. Facing Jonah, he extended a hand, palm out. "Son, you best go somewhere and cool off."

Caleb looked around, saw Zoe stop stirring a pot, saw Chloe frowning, saw Mariah take Zeke by the hand. "Come now, let's have us a little excursion."

"No, Mariah!" yelled Jonah. "You stay and hear this thing out."

Mariah stopped in her tracks but kept her back to Jonah.

"I ask you one more time!" Jonah was breathing hard. "Say what kind you were!"

"I think I'll be saying good night." Caleb headed for the wagon.

"You stand and answer me!" Jonah shoved Mordecai aside, grabbed Caleb by the collar, then punched him in the face. Caleb's hat went flying. His body crashed into the wagon.

Mariah spun around. "Jonah, what in the world is wrong with you?"

Balance back, Caleb snatched up one of the fence rails in the wagon, raised it, then let it drop. He put his hand to his left cheek, winced, picked up his hat from the ground.

Mordecai again stepped between Jonah and Caleb. Zoe and Chloe rushed over. Hagar and others camped nearby gathered around.

"Nothin' wrong with me," shouted Jonah. "It's him!" He pointed at Caleb, then jabbed at the air with each word. "I say he was a driver!"

Hagar gasped. "Driver? He was a driver?"

Caleb backed away as others within earshot came over. He guessed that most in the crowd had never known of a driver who wasn't a low-down, dirty dog, a traitor to his people. Short-changed people on rations. Lied on people so they'd get the lash.

Hagar scurried over to the wagon, grabbed a fence rail meant for firewood, made it a menace. She thumped the ground. "Driver!"

Others reached for fence rails, thumped the ground too.

"Driver! Driver! Driver!" they chanted. Some just stamped their feet. "Driver! Driver! Driver!" The crowd swelled.

Caleb looked around, confounded, as the people closed in.

Hagar in the dress he'd provided.

Hosea holding the banjo he'd found for him.

Even Ben in the pants and waistcoat he'd provided.

Rachel, Jedidiah, Effie, John, Leah, Elisha, Carrie, Tom, Bill, Emmanuel, Emmaline, and a host whose names he didn't know—Caleb had done most all of them good turns along the way. But none of it meant anything now. Worst of all was the look on Mariah's face.

Caleb saw a flicker of heartbreak, a flash of sorrow. *Does she truly think I was a driver?*

"Have y'all lost your minds?" Caleb shouted.

"Driver! Driver! Driver!"

"I wasn't no driver! I swear!"

Mordecai stepped in. "Hagar, Hosea, everybody, just calm down now. Go about your business."

"I don't believe him!" fumed Jonah.

"Jonah! That's enough!" cried Chloe.

"I swear, Jonah," said Caleb calmly. "I wasn't no driver. Don't know how you ever got such a notion."

"You got bossman ways about you!" Jonah yelled.

"No driver, Jonah."

Jonah turned to the crowd. "Y'all notice he got a quality of clothing not like the rest of us?"

"Amen to that!" somebody called out.

"Y'all see how he friendly with Yankees?" Jonah was shouting now.

"Seen it!" somebody else called out.

"Driver! Driver! Driver!"

The crowd had grown larger.

Caleb feared for his life—he had to put the fire out now. "I couldn't have been a driver, people!" he shouted. "I wasn't a slave. I was born free."

"Order!" Captain Galloway roared. "Order!" He was on his bay steed. Privates Sykes and Dolan, both clean-shaven, trotted behind him.

"Order!" Captain Galloway shouted again. He pointed at Jonah. "Take that man away. Put him in the stocks!" Then to the crowd: "We have trouble enough with the Rebels," he said. "We need no trouble from the colored."

Caleb watched Hagar and the others hurry back to their campsites. Mordecai and the Doubles only stepped back. Mariah didn't move. Now it wasn't heartbreak and sorrow that Caleb saw on Mariah's face, but shock. Anger too.

Caleb stepped over to Captain Galloway. "A word, sir?"

Captain Galloway nodded.

"No harm was really done here."

"Really?" said Captain Galloway, inspecting Caleb's eye.

"Just a small misunderstanding."

"Small misunderstanding?"

"Yes, sir," Caleb replied, looking Galloway eye to eye. "My fault."

Up jumped Zeke. He hurried over, pulled on the captain's coat. All smiles, he offered a salute.

Caleb knew Captain Galloway didn't want to put Jonah in the stocks. He had done it once to a colored man outside Atlanta, punishment for trying to steal a rifle. "Made me feel like a filthy slaveholder," the captain later told Caleb. And now Caleb could see that the captain was looking to maintain order and save face.

"Privates Sykes, Private Dolan," said Captain Galloway, "first take him to my tent for interrogation."

"Thank you, sir," Caleb whispered.

When Galloway rode away, Caleb looked around and saw people stealing glances at him, guilty looks on their faces.

And Mariah was gone.

Tightrope Walker

"Did you know Caleb was always free?" asked Chloe over supper.

"No," Mariah replied, head down, embarrassed.

"I'm sure he kept it from you for a good reason," said Mordecai.

But what possible reason could he have had? Mariah asked herself. She couldn't help but feel betrayed, made a fool of, even.

After supper Chloe handed her a sliced-up potato in a bandana and Zoe a small kettle filled with soup.

"You should go see about him," said Chloe.

"I'm sure he's fine," replied Mariah.

"What did I say?" Chloe had her hands on her hips now.

Mariah relented, realizing that a small part of her did

wonder how Caleb was faring. But more than that, she wanted answers.

She walked from group to group, bandana in one hand, kettle in the other.

"Up thataway," somebody said.

"Cross yonder," another told her.

The wind was at her back when she found Caleb sitting outside his tent. Like every night before, a thousand campfires were crackling.

"Why you never told me?"

His shrug hurt.

"Captain Galloway know?"

Caleb nodded.

That hurt worse. After all she'd shared with him. She handed Caleb the kettle, the bandana, and got furious when he barely looked up.

"The less they know about me, the more I learn. If they think I was a slave, I'm invisible, I'm—"

"Like cattle? Like me?"

"That's not what I meant."

Somewhere in the darkness, a man sang "Go Down, Moses."

"Caleb, I thought we were . . ."

He looked up. "What?"

Mariah looked away. "Well, friends. But now it's like I don't even know you."

"Some soldiers likely to think a free man uppity. Could make me a target."

"But *me*? I'm no Yankee soldier."

"Didn't want it to get out. After I told Galloway I regretted it."

"But *me*? You didn't trust *me*, Caleb? You trusted that white man more than me?"

"It wasn't so much that I was trusting him. It just slipped out."

A saw-whet owl *hoot-hoot*ed.

"I was planning to tell you."

"When?"

"Was waiting for the right time."

"Why wasn't it the right time when I told you about my pa, my ma? Why wasn't it the right time when—"

"Nothing's changed, Mariah. I'm still the same man. Whether I was a slave or always free, what's changed?" He unwrapped the bandana, put a potato slice to his left cheek.

"We from different places, different worlds."

"We both colored. We both Southern born. Besides, you're free now."

Mariah waited for him to go on, explain himself, but all he gave her was silence.

Along with being angry, Mariah now also felt a tinge of guilt. Back when people were about to mob Caleb, for a split second she had wavered, remembering what Jonah had said the day they left the Chaney place. *Any colored man got common ground with a white man gotta be a hazard to the rest of us.* Yes, for an instant she had doubted Caleb, thinking if he had been a driver that explained why he talked more about the march than himself.

And perhaps Caleb had seen her doubt.

Mariah sat down across from him. "What was it like?" She had never met a free colored person.

Now someone was playing a ditty on a reed pipe.

"Ever been to the circus?" Caleb asked.

"Once." Mariah thought about that one precious day she saw a talking horse, a jester, tiny people juggling. "Years ago. With money ma made from her garden."

"Was there a tightrope walker?"

Mariah stared into the fire as Caleb told her about white guardians to vouch for free colored, about free papers, kidnappings. "Over us hung a fear that if we were ever caught without our papers, we'd wind up on an auction block in New Orleans. Never let our guard down when not among just our own."

"Your own bein' other free colored?" All this time what she thought was care—was it all just pity? When he looked at her, did he only see damage?

"Our own being colored people, free and slave. Like I said, Mariah, we both colored, both Southern born, and now both free."

"Soup's goin' cold."

"Will heat it up in the morning, have it for breakfast."

An awkward silence followed.

Caleb was the first to speak. "Look, Mariah, my pa spent twenty-six years in slavery. Most colored in and around Atlanta was in slavery, some of them kin. So it's not like I lived in ignorance before I met you."

That stung and surprised her too. Mariah had assumed that . . . "How did your pa get free?"

"His skills and good fortune."

Mariah thought for a bit. "A blacksmith?"

Caleb nodded. "His fences, gates, railings—all of such fine quality, patterns of charm, grace—he never had trouble getting work. Most of his customers were big planters."

"This after he got free?"

"Before and after. When a slave, he was allowed to hire himself out. Had to give his owner fifty dollars a month. All above that was his to keep. This was in Decatur."

Mariah saw pride rising in Caleb when he told her how his father scrimped and saved for freedom. "Cost him eighteen hundred dollars, and he had enough left over to buy a few acres right outside Atlanta. Built a nice-sized house, work-shop out back."

"Why didn't he go North?"

Caleb stared at Mariah for a while, then said, "Because a fine young lady named Rebecca Baker wasn't North."

Mariah smiled. She knew where the story was going. "Your ma?"

Caleb nodded. "She and her family were freed years earlier. Owner got true religion. Anyhow, her family ran a secondhand clothing shop in Atlanta. That's where Pa first laid eyes on her. Knew at first sight that she was the one. After he got himself set, he went about courting the apple of his eye."

"And was he the apple of her eye?"

Caleb leaned back on his elbow. His eyes danced. "Ma always said Pa had been coming around the shop for weeks before she paid him a wisp of attention. Then Pa, he'd stroke her face and say, 'Becky, you know you loved me right off,' and she'd say, 'Jacob Drew, you stop being so full of yourself.' Then they'd laugh and let the story lie."

"Did your pa really love your ma from the moment he first saw her?"

"That's what he said. And Pa wasn't one to trifle."

"And your ma, you think it took her a while?"

"I tend to think not."

Mariah found herself lingering a little too long in Caleb's eyes. When she looked away, she scratched a spot on her neck that didn't itch.

"Could be your ma took to your pa at first sight, just like

he did her, but she just wanted to wait a bit. Make sure he was a good man."

Caleb sat up and tossed a pine knot on the fire, looked directly into Mariah's eyes. "You think my ma wasn't smart enough to know a good man when she saw one?"

Mariah scratched a place on her forearm that didn't itch. "I'm sure your ma was plenty smart, Caleb," she finally said. "Most likely she just wanted to make sure. Have some extra guarantee. Maybe she didn't want to let on at first how she felt for fear he'd change his mind."

"My pa wasn't the changeable type."

"But your ma didn't know that."

Caleb laughed. "You got a point there." He rubbed his hands before the fire. "Whatever was holding Ma back, it didn't last long. They married two weeks after he gave her a gold double locket on a neck chain."

"What was in the locket?"

"Nothing. Both sides empty. He asked her if she could ever see the locket with a portrait of him on one side and her on the other. As husband and wife."

"And she said yes?"

"What do you think?"

Mariah looked down sheepishly, feeling a bit silly. Somewhat giddy too.

Caleb undid the top buttons of his shirt, took from around his neck a locket on a chain, and handed it to Mariah.

She hesitated.

"Go on," he urged.

Mariah wiped her hands on her dress before taking it. Carefully, she opened the locket, stared in awe at the two photographs. Woman on the left. Man on the right. Both in fancy black.

Mariah saw that Caleb had his father's cheekbones and jaw. Same broad shoulders.

Caleb's eyes and his full lips were like his ma's.

Fine color came from both. Pa like velvet midnight. Ma only a tad lighter.

"They look so prosperous and so happy." She closed the locket, handed it back to Caleb. "You fortunate to have a keepsake like that. Only likenesses I got of my folks is what I hold in my head."

Just then Mariah realized that she had failed to stay mad at Caleb. The anger, the hurt, it had all drifted away like dry leaves whisked away by a breeze. Even more unsettling—and scary—was that Mariah found herself wondering what it would be like to give Caleb her grace, and she found herself knowing that he was her somewhere place.

But she thought it best to shift her mind to something else. Mariah puzzled for a bit. If Caleb was on the march, his folks must be dead. No matter how wrecked Atlanta was, if they were still alive, she couldn't see him leaving them behind.

"Your folks? Both gone?"

He nodded. "Pa right before the war broke out, passed in his sleep. Ma went earlier this year."

Mariah saw that Caleb no longer wanted to talk about his folks.

"You the only child?"

"Yep." After a pause Caleb said, "Only one to survive. Some died as babies and—"

Caleb's jaw tightened.

"And what?"

"Had a sister, Lily. She died earlier this year too. Was only thirteen."

Caleb's whole mood had changed. He looked in pain.

Had his sister and mother been taken by consumption? Winter fever?

Now was not the time to ask, she decided. "I should turn in," she said.

She didn't want to leave, hoped Caleb would ask her to stay a little longer.

Those words never came.

OFFERED HIM A CHOCOLATE

For Friday, December 2, 1864, Caleb jotted down that the division had moved out at daybreak, that the march had been zigzagging.

What a jangled day it had been. "Pvt. L. who went missing 2 days ago was found dead. More things are breaking. Wheels. Wagons. Tent poles. Limber chests. Men." Caleb wrote about the picket guard who took leave of his senses in the middle of the night. The Irishman had ripped off all his clothes and jabbered about Judgment Day.

"J. attacked me this evening & tried to loose others on me, claiming I was a driver. I had to let out that I was born free so as not to be killed." Caleb admitted that for a split second he relished the thought of Jonah in the stocks, but then he realized that if he didn't intercede on Jonah's behalf then he really was no better than a driver. "Capt. G. said when he had J. in his tent, he looked very sorry and said as much. For that,

Capt. G. offered him a chocolate. When J. asked a favor, Capt. G. obliged him."

Caleb wished he had had some chocolate or other treat to offer Mariah when she came to his tent. The hurt and anger in her eyes grieved him. "At one point I thought she might throw the soup in my face. But she gentled down, went back to her sweet self. And now she knows how I came to be free, some things about my folks. I told her of Lily, but only that she was dead. Camped near Waynesboro."

Till We Meet Again

"You don't need to do this, Jonah."

"Yeah, Mariah, I do."

"But where will you go?" asked Chloe.

"Asked Captain Galloway to get me on to the pioneers."

Chloe shook her head. "We'll hardly ever see you."

"I'll keep in touch through the grapevine." Jonah lifted a sack from the ground, slung it across a shoulder. Eyes on the ground, he said, "I'm real sorry for the strife."

Mordecai rose from a half barrel, patted Jonah on the shoulder. "None of us perfect. Owning up is a giant step."

Mariah's stomach was in knots from the guilt. Had she never told Jonah "maybe" back when they were on the Chaney place, none of this would have happened. "Jonah, I'm sorry I—"

"No, Mariah, you did nothin' wrong. Only told the truth."

"But there's no cause for you to go." Mariah fought back tears. "Things will smooth over."

"As I see it," said Jonah, "I'll be gettin' myself ready for full freedom. Learnin' to build roads, bridges. Skills should put me in good stead wherever we—wherever I settle."

Zeke sat cross-legged beside Mordecai. "Jonah go?"

Dulcina, sitting beside Zeke, looked up. "Texas?"

"No, Miss Dulcina, not Texas, not that far." Jonah squatted down next to Zeke. "That's right, little man, Jonah go." He removed his muffler from around his neck, put it around the boy's, then said to Mordecai, "That other sack, will you mind it for me, please?"

"Will do," replied Mordecai.

"And if . . . if we get lost to each other, y'all split it up fairly."

"We won't lose each other!" Mariah insisted. "There's the grapevine, like you said."

Zoe handed Jonah some breakfast wrapped in a bandana. Johnnycake and cracklins.

Jonah nodded his thanks. "I thank all y'all for your goodness to me over the years." Jonah reached into his breast pocket and handed Mordecai, then the Doubles, then Mariah a twenty-dollar gold piece.

Zoe arched an eyebrow, Chloe gasped, Mordecai ran a hand over his head.

"I'll explain later," said Mariah.

"Y'all the only family I got left." Jonah wiped his eyes. "Tell Caleb I hope he can forgive." Jonah put his hat on his head. "Till we meet again," he said.

"Till we meet again," said Chloe, Zoe, and Mordecai.

Mariah closed her hand around the gold coin out of regard for the giver. She tippy-toed up, gave Jonah a kiss on the cheek. "Till we meet again."

FAMILY

Caleb was of two minds about Jonah joining the pioneers. On the one hand, it put an end to the friction. It would, he hoped, also ease Jonah's pining for Mariah. Caleb knew how he would feel if he couldn't have her heart. And last night he knew he did. There was something in the way she looked at him when they talked about his folks' courtship.

But Mariah had known Jonah all her life. In time would she come to resent Caleb for the separation—even though it hadn't been his fault? Every time she looked at him would she be reminded of losing Jonah?

Only temporary, Caleb told himself. At the end of the march there'd be a reuniting. *Lord,* he said to himself, *don't let Jonah get hurt—or worse—while a pioneer.*

Caleb was on his way to see Jonah that morning, to tell him no hard feelings and urge him not to go. When he saw Mariah and the others huddled around Jonah, he stopped in his tracks.

He was too far away to hear what they were saying, but he could see anew how very much they were family. A family forced and forged under slavery's brutal reign, but a family nonetheless.

What he'd give to have a family again. What he'd give to be part of this family. Husband to Mariah. Father to Zeke. Maybe even work into a bygones-be-bygones brotherhood with Jonah. Keep Mordecai and the Doubles close for fatherly and motherly advice. Keep Dulcina close, too, because it was the right thing to do.

When Caleb saw Mariah give Jonah a kiss on the cheek, he felt he had no right to approach, interrupt their sad and tender parting. Caleb also thought it best if he kept his distance that evening.

Night Became a Wishing Well

Mariah stayed on the lookout for Caleb that evening. When they camped. When they supped. When she got the tent up. She could understand why he made himself scarce what with the way folks had ganged up against him on Jonah's wild say, but didn't he want to see her? She had only laid eyes on him once that day, at the Buckhead Creek crossing. But he said not a word to her. Just helped.

With Zeke in the tent, tucked in with his pouch of peppermint sticks and his timberdoodle, Mariah sat alone by the fire. Missing Caleb. Jonah too.

She wondered, hoped, second-guessed. None of it did a bit of good. She finally gave up and joined a gathering around a bonfire.

Mordecai beside Chloe. Between her and Zoe, Dulcina curled up in a ball. Effie, who had joined the march outside Louisville, made room for Mariah between herself and Zoe.

Hagar was telling of what she called her "all-time scariest meet-up with a haint." The ghost was swooping down, she said, when her brother cried out, "'Quick, turn your pockets inside out!' Quick, I did, and that haint wizened into vapor!"

Some in the gathering seemed frightened. Others not much.

"Dead can't do us no harm," said Effie. "Seen plenty o' haints in my time. All on the playful side. None never done me harm. All my hurts and pains come from the livin'."

"Amen," said Hosea, after a puff on his pipe.

Mariah felt a growing tension in the air. *Like me, they all have scars*, she thought. *Like me, they all have terrors to tell.*

"My whitefolks was both devils," testified Dessa from Davisboro. "Come Christmas warn't no use chillun scamper to the Big House shoutin' 'Christmas gif'! Christmas gif'!' Git they ears boxed is all."

Mariah recalled Christmases past, days when the Chaneys had everybody head to the Big House back door for bounty. Dried Fruits. Fresh meat. New shoes. Cloth. As a child, Christmas after Christmas, she believed that the Chaneys' gifts were a sign of a softening of their hearts.

She remembered, too, Christmas merriment in the quarters. Her pa playing his fiddle—fast-time tunes during these days. Her ma shake, shake, shaking her gourd rattle. Others strumming banjos, blowing the quills. And ancient Aunt Minda patting her feet, bobbing her head, ancient Aunt Minda who beguiled her, Jonah, and the other children with tales of a village far, far away in a land called Guinea, tales she'd been told as a child and told to pass on. Along with the stories of frisky spiders and big cats getting spots, Aunt Minda sometimes taught little Mariah and other children words from Guinea.

Aban—Strength! *Akoben*—Devotion! *Akofena*—Courage! *Sankofa*—Remember!

Mariah remembered boundless cheer at Christmastide until they were made to gather outside and listen to that preacher with a fire-and-brimstone mind. "The Four Horsemen of the Apocalypse be War, Famine, Disease, and Death!"

"We call it the killin' stone." Those words wrenched Mariah back from memories. Effie again. "We call it the killin' stone," she repeated, rocking slowly, eyes on the fire.

Effie told of a rock outcrop on the edge of her town, of white women snatching light-skinned babies from black women's arms. "Them white women cuss up the colored women somethin' awful. Scratch, kick, slap. Act like the colored women had a power to keep massas off 'em." Effie wiped her eyes. "Them white women bash colored babies' brains out on the killin' stone. Sometime they hurl the little bodies into the bush, sometime just drop 'em right there by the stone. Howsoever us could, us sneak and bury. Warn't right to leave 'em for varmints to devour."

Across from Mariah, a woman new to the march began sobbing. "Was sold from place to place when young on account of I couldn't bear no children. Each time farther away from my folks."

"Take your time, take your time," said Mordecai softly as Miriam struggled to tell about the bloodhounds unleashed on her brother. The boy had been caught sneaking a ham from the smokehouse, then he fought back when the driver tried to whip him. "D-d-d-dawgs t-t-t-tow the flesh fr-fr-fr-from m-m-m-mah br-br-br-brutha buh-buh-bones."

Copper-skinned Ben held up his right hand with its forefinger missing the first joint.

"Tried to learn your letters?" asked Mariah.

Ben nodded.

"Beastly people." Rachel sighed, circling one arm around her little Rose, one hand spread on her big belly.

A nighthawk cawed. Mordecai rose, tossed a few fence rails onto the fire, returned to Chloe's side.

"We was born in Virginia." She sniffled.

Mariah turned, saw Chloe with her head lowered, saw Mordecai patting her hand, saw Zoe swallow.

"Was six years old when Doc Melrose's father paid a visit. His wife took a shine to us. Given they important folk, our master—" Chloe took a deep breath, stroked Dulcina's arm. "Night before we was to go, our mama fixed on our memories." Chloe paused again. "Mama said, 'You Zoe and Chloe from Richmond, Virginia.' Then she had us say it back to her three times."

From off a ways came a squeal. Like a rabbit in an owl's talons.

"Next, Mama said, 'You born on James Carter place.' We repeated that three times."

Zoe sniffled.

"Then she said, 'Your mama named Ruth. She second cook on the Carter place.'"

Zoe reached over Dulcina, took her sister's other hand.

"Your daddy named—" Chloe began to sob.

Zoe, fighting back tears, picked up where her sister left off. "Your daddy named William. He a wheelwright and cooper on the Carter place."

Chloe spoke on. "You got five brothers and sisters—"

Zoe spoke on. "Hannah, Daniel, Phoebe, Cyrus, Peter."

"Come morning," continued Chloe, "after Mama and Daddy hugged us hard, Mama asked if we remember the lesson. We was too crying to speak, so we nod. She pat our heads, hold us tight one last time, then told us to keep remembering because"—Chloe took a deep breath—"because every good-bye ain't gone." After another pause, she added through tears, "That was nearly—"

"Fifty years ago," Zoe finished up, wiping her eyes.

Mariah was stunned. She had never heard their story, never seen the Doubles cry, never known them to put an ounce of pain on display. And now there was a glistening in Mordecai's eyes.

"At ten I was made playmate to Miss Callie's brother, taught to groom the boy's pony, groom the boy." Mordecai paused. "Was a cruel boy. Used to saddle me with a collar, leash, make me walk on all fours." Mordecai paused again. "Time and again my pa looked on in pain when he was out there trimming hedges, pruning roses, weeding, swinging the scythe across the lawn. For Pa's sake I tried to keep my tears inside."

Mariah saw Chloe squeeze Mordecai's hand.

"There were times he couldn't do the same when the boy was abusing me. Also when he heard Miss Callie's mother or father cuss my mama, smack her around. Was a horrible thing to see my pa cry."

Mariah saw Chloe rub Mordecai's back.

"One night I found my pa in the garden, weeping a river. 'I ain't a man. I ain't a man,' he kept saying." Mordecai swallowed. "I helped him to our cabin, cheered him up some with a hand-shadow show, went to bed plum proud that I'd saved Pa from a consuming sorrow."

Mariah was by now on the verge of tears herself.

"Turns out all I'd done was fool myself." Mordecai's voice quivered. "In the middle of the night, Pa slipped from the cabin and hanged himself in the livery."

Rachel shook her head. "Poor man."

Mordecai took a deep breath. "On that day I made a pledge. Never take a wife. Never sire a child, not so long as I'm bound.

Kept the pledge when a young valet. Kept the pledge when Miss Callie, off and married, wrote to her father begging for me, saying none of the judge's colored men had the quality to be a butler."

Chloe wrapped her arms around Mordecai. Mariah heard him whisper, "Now you know why."

"And to think," said Della, "some of them shocked to see us take off with the Yanks." Della, a high yalla, angular woman with a patch over her right eye, had joined the march only a few hours before. With her was a grizzled, old, humpbacked man, her father, Gus.

Mariah soon learned that Callie Chaney was hardly the only one to give out scare talk about the Yanks.

A woman named Nannie recalled her owner telling her that before the Yanks set fire to buildings in Atlanta, they locked up hundreds of colored people inside them.

"We was told self-same story," whispered Rachel.

Ben cleared his throat. "Massa told me Yanks drowned all the colored women and children in the Chattahoochee."

"Them devils say anything to keep us bound," muttered Mordecai.

"And the Bible say the devil is a liar!" Hagar roared.

"So many Yanks been mighty kind," said Rachel.

With that, talk turned to individual bluecoats. Thoughts, observations, news picked up while cooking, herding, laundering, blacking boots. There was talk of the ones who tickled them, like the burly sergeant who went about slapping younger soldiers on the back and exclaiming, "Prave boys! Such prave boys!"

"That's Sergeant Hoffmann," said Mariah.

"Ones like him," said Mordecai. "They from Germany."

"That near New York?" someone asked.

"No, across an ocean. In Europe."

"They have slavery over there?" asked Ben.

"No, they do not," Mordecai replied.

Hosea recalled Sergeant Hoffmann handing out pants and caps. Hagar spoke about Private Sykes handing out socks. Rachel remembered Private Dolan bringing baskets for laundry.

"You know it's Captain Galloway behind their goodness," said Chloe.

"Captain Galloway, he's the king of kindness," added Mariah.

The captain had supped with them that night. It had been a one-pot meal of cowpeas, rice, and pork.

"Most delicious!" he said after his first forkful. "What flavor!" he exclaimed. "I taste the . . . hot pepper . . . onion, and . . . ?" He looked at Zoe.

A tightlipped smile was all he got back by way of a reply.

"Go on." Captain Galloway smiled back. "Aren't you going to tell me the rest of the ingredients?"

"Well, sir, if I tell you, sir, all the fine flavor will fade away."

Captain Galloway wagged his finger. "I've heard how you cooks guard your recipes," he said. "But you know, you might want to give up some of your secrets. There's money to be made in a cookbook. An uncle of mine has a small publishing company. I could make an introduction after, well, you know, when we get through all this."

Mariah was stunned to see the captain acting like he was with his own. Was something wrong with him? He didn't smell like he'd been drinking.

"And your cookbook," Captain Galloway continued after another forkful, "it might just become a calling card for a catering business. You might even open a restaurant. I have some friends who might back such an endeavor."

Is he crazy? Mariah couldn't recall a white person having a conversation with a colored person. She remembered plenty of talk—

Fetch me a sherry, then draw my bath!

Yes, ma'am.

Can't churn faster than that?

Yes, ma'am.

Have Jack butcher that hog Friday next!

Yes, sir.

Put the kettle on!

Yes, ma'am.

Send for Reuben!

Yes, ma'am.

That silver better have a mirror shine!

Yes, ma'am.

Where the blazes is Reuben?

Don't know, ma'am.

Talk. Never conversation, like Captain Galloway was making, being more than kind, being friendly.

They had just sat down to eat when the captain came over. When they stopped, stood up, he bid them take their seats.

Awkward smile on his face, hands clasped behind his back, he rocked on his heels.

"Something we can do for you, sir?" Mordecai had asked.

"Oh no. I just, just came to see how you all are faring."

"Right fine," replied Mordecai.

"Having supper?" The captain rubbed his hands.

"Yes, sir."

"Looks good."

"Would you like some, sir?" asked Mariah.

"Yes, I would—if you have some to spare."

Mariah rose. "Zeke, give me your cup."

The captain tensed. Was he afraid to eat behind colored? No, she soon found out. It wasn't that.

"I wouldn't dare take the child's food!" he said.

"Don't trouble yourself, sir," said Mariah. "I can put his in my cup—he can eat from mine. I'll just give his cup a little wash up for your portion." Mariah lifted the lid from the pot. "See, there's plenty more."

Mariah watched Galloway peer into the pot, then get a fix

on the beat-up tin half skillet Mordecai ate from, the Doubles' dented dipper cups, her and Zeke's tin cups. Dulcina, her back to the group, wasn't eating at all.

"No need," said Galloway. "Please, Mariah, sit back down. Let your brother keep his cup. I'll be *right* back," which Mariah knew would be true, for this night, the captain camped closer to the colored than to his comrades.

"Well, I never," said Chloe when the captain was out of range.

"That is one peculiar man," added Mordecai.

When Captain Galloway returned, Mariah eyed his tin plate, a strange long mahogany case with a brass shield and a silver cap. She had seen other soldiers' eating ware, what Caleb had told her were called mess kits, but she'd never seen any as marvelous as the captain's. Inside the case was a fork, spoon, and knife with fancy black handles. There was also a corkscrew and a strange little contraption. The case's silver cap she realized doubled as a cup.

"Salt and pepper anyone?" asked the captain, unscrewing the little contraption and revealing two shakers.

As he supped, Captain Galloway seemed to be enjoying every forkful.

"And what is this dish called?" he asked at one point.

"Hoppin' John," replied Zoe.

"Hahpin—"

"Think of a boy named John, sir," said Mordecai. "Then see that boy hop."

"Oh," said Galloway. "Hopping John."

"Yes, sir," said Mordecai.

"And why, pray tell, is it called hopping John?"

"No idea, sir."

Before Captain Galloway left he gave Mordecai his tin plate and mess kit.

"Oh no, sir, I couldn't possibly take your things," Mordecai protested, but the captain insisted.

"Captain Galloway, he's the king of kindness," Mariah said again, later that night during the bonfire gathering. She looked over at the captain bundled up in his overcoat, warming his hands by a small campfire.

"Captain Galloway, sir!" Mordecai called out. "You should know a host of us pray you up every day!" Standing at his full height, Mordecai gave the captain a salute.

Captain Galloway returned the salute.

"We pray for all the good Yanks!" Effie hollered out. "Sherman on down."

"I heard Sherman insane," whispered Hagar.

"Aw, stop that now," said Mordecai, shaking his head.

Nannie looked over one shoulder, then the other. "Is odd how he go about more like vagabond than ginral. Black hat half-covering his face, ratty brown overcoat like—"

"Ever get a close look at his face?" interrupted Hagar.

"Not close," someone replied.

"Red hair tussled up," said Hagar. "Pale eyes jump all over. Face like a skirmish."

"That's the truth," said Mariah. The few times she'd laid eyes on Sherman his face was a scowl.

"Don't much sleep, I hear," added Lovie. "Deep in the night, up a-walkin' an' a-walkin'.'"

"Sound like he haunted," said Hagar.

"Ghost of his son." That was Hosea's guess. "Heard it only been about a year since the little fella died."

"Boy must be comin' to him in his sleep," insisted Hagar. "That's why he walk the night."

"Could be the son's death is what made Sherman crazy," offered Ben.

"Crazy or not," Mordecai weighed in, "if not for Sherman we wouldn't be on the freedom road right now. I say if crazy make a man bring wreck and ruin to secesh and freedom to us, we all need to pray every hour for a hundred more crazy General Shermans."

"And no more General Rebs!" declared Mariah. She knew that if some thought Sherman was crazy, they all saw Jefferson Davis in Union blue as a son of ole slewfoot, evil shot-through. "Put nothin' past that man," she said. "Not after what he did today."

"What happened?" asked Gus.

"Before we all could get across," explained Hagar, "soldiers pulled up that newfangled bridge they got."

"It's called a pontoon," said Mariah. "Pontoon bridge."

"Did it on General Reb's say is what we heard."

"And who is General Reb?" the newcomer asked.

"Evilest Yank in the world," replied Hosea. "Was him, they say, ordered the bridge pulled up. Left us to slosh our way across."

"If anybody deserve a hauntin', it's Ginral Reb," said Hagar. "And I don't mean no playful haints."

"They say five or six of our people drowned," added Mariah.

"Some turned back," said Hosea.

Hagar frowned. "Lord knows what they up against now."

Mariah could see that Mordecai didn't like things going gloomy again. "People, let us cease from talk of evil," he said. "I say it's time to speak of our dreams, our new tomorrows."

Mariah looked around. Everyone seemed adrift.

Caws of a nighthawk came and went.

Mariah wondered if anyone would dare speak of dreams, of a new tomorrow, what with nothing certain. After a few more nighthawks cawed away, to Mariah's surprise, the night became a wishing well.

Sleep in a proper bed . . . Sleep till noon for just one day . . . Find my sister . . . Find my daughters . . . Get my little ones some learnin' . . . Learn my letters . . . Weeklong barbecue! . . . Get my picture took . . . Shoes that fit my feet . . . Be lazy one whole day . . . Fair money for my labor . . . Go to a real church . . . Brick house . . . Become a soldier . . . Go to Europe . . .

"Have shops side by side," said Zoe. "Eating house. Healing house."

Mordecai squeezed Chloe's hand.

"What about you, Mariah?" asked Hagar.

Mariah looked up. "I hope to get my brother some help."

"But for you, what you want for you?" asked Ben.

Caleb. Mariah didn't dare say that out loud. But there was one thing she'd always wanted whenever she fixed her mind on freedom. She fingered the tiny sling sack she'd made for the gold coin from Jonah, a sack tacked in her apron pocket.

"My own ground," she said sheepishly. "Don't need to be a lot. I'd be content with one acre. One acre with good soil for growing our food. One acre near a fine fishing spot. One acre to call my own. My own ground."

RELISH IN DESTRUCTION

"Division moved at 7. Made 10 miles," began Caleb's entry for Saturday, December 3, 1864. "We passed through Millen."

The more Caleb thought about what he wanted to do after the war, the more he thought of his diary becoming a book. He doubted that many of his people on the march could write, and he was certain that a load of Yankees would write articles or books about the march. He'd bet money that most would give colored short shrift.

"Did Jack tell you about those monkey-like pickaninnies?" That's what he'd heard one private tell another when he returned from Social Circle.

It sickened Caleb the way some soldiers mocked his people, making them sound so ignorant. Like the lieutenant who told of happening upon a toothless old man, shouting, "I is off to Glory!"

Back when they marched through Milledgeville there was

the colonel who had several soldiers in stitches with his tale of encountering a group of "greasy black wenches" living in boxcars.

The darkies this. The darkies that. Caleb couldn't count the times when, while repairing a wheel, shoeing a horse, or packing a wagon he had to bite his tongue, keep his head down, pretend to be nothing but a simple darkie himself.

If Captain Galloway, Sergeant Hoffmann, or a few other Yankees who treated him like a man wrote about the march, Caleb knew his people wouldn't be presented as beasts and buffoons. But if they didn't, the world would never know how much the colored on the march endured, never know the brains and brawn they gave to the march—all their labors, all the intelligence on treasure hiding places, Rebel militiamen, geography. The more Caleb thought about it, the more he truly wanted to make his diary the basis of a book. For that, he'd need to write in more detail about everything.

On the night of December 3, he wrote about the shock the Yankees got when they reached Camp Lawton, right outside Millen. "Yankees hoped to liberate about 8,000 Union men from that prison camp. When they got there they found the place deserted. Sgt. H. said there were corpses strewn about aboveground and hundreds buried in a mass grave. The hovels prisoners were forced to live in weren't fit for a dog, he said. Gen. W.T.S. ordered Gen. F.B. to make Millen a wasteland. Sgt. H. said all that is left of Millen, from its depot to its hotel, are ashes. Yankees also burned Camp Lawton.

Capt. G. told me he fears that too many Union soldiers are taking too lusty a relish in destruction."

Caleb gave his pencil a shaving. Then he recorded what happened at Buckhead Creek.

He had crossed earlier in the day to be on hand for repairs as wagons reached the other side. When he heard about the bridge being pulled up before all the colored crossed, he hurried to their rescue. "About a dozen Yanks, Pvts. S. & D. among them, also helped. Miss C. lost some of her herbs. Z. his cap. Mord. his hat. After I helped at the crossing I kept clear of M. and the rest. Camped at Lumpkin Station."

TEXAS

Mariah awoke in a sweat, breathing hard. Scraps of a nightmare drifted around her mind. When she came clear—saw she wasn't back at the Chaney place but in the tent—she breathed a sigh of relief. A few seconds later—panic.

"What happened?" Chloe rubbed sleep from her eyes.

Mariah had a dress on, was reaching for her shoes. "Dulcina! She's gone!"

"Good Lord!" Chloe gasped.

When Mariah saw Chloe moving to get dressed, she said, "No, you stay here! Mind Zeke."

"Zoe can do that." Chloe stirred her sister. "You can't be going about on your own."

"I'll get Mordecai."

"Three heads are better than two."

* * *

If only she hadn't slept so hard, Mariah chided herself as they searched for five minutes, ten minutes, fifteen, around a host of other campsites, in the woods, near a stream.

In the predawn light they finally found her in the brambles, up on a knoll near a copse of loblolly trees.

Neck broken. Dress, torn in places, up about her waist. A Union blue cap stuffed in her mouth. Cold eyes stared into gone tomorrows. Before heading back with the grim news, Mariah pulled down Dulcina's dress. Chloe closed her eyes.

Mariah was hollowed out, couldn't cry.

Digging the shallow grave.

Caleb making a cross from a fence rail.

Mordecai saying a few words, then leading them in prayer. Still Mariah didn't cry.

When she looked up from prayer, she saw Captain Galloway approaching.

"I will launch an investigation," he said, his face so solemn.

"Thank you, sir," said Mariah. Still she had not cried.

Back at their campsite, Mariah declined the bit of breakfast Hagar and Rachel had put together for them. No taste even for a cup of coffee.

What should she tell Zeke, who was sitting in Rachel's lap nibbling a biscuit.

If only Caleb didn't have to ride out. She didn't just want him. She needed him. But all that morning he hardly said a word to anybody, including her. And why did he look so . . . it was more than sorrow. It was the same look that came over him when he told her about his sister, Lily, being dead.

As Mariah watched Caleb head off with Captain Galloway, her mind wound back to that first big meet-up in the quarters when the war began. With Nero out cold from corn liquor, they had gathered in Aunt Minda's cabin. They whispered what they heard, thought, hoped.

Aunt Minda, blind and with her joints locked up from rheumatism, just listened, bundled up in her bed.

After Jack, Josie, Sadie, Esther, Maceo, Upson, Paul, Flora, Reuben, Nate, Mordecai, Jonah, and everybody else had their say, only then did Aunt Minda speak. Whatever she foresaw, they would believe.

A candle in the middle of the floor flickered.

"Git ready . . . ," Aunt Minda said, voice raspy, rattly. "Freedom dawnin'." She raised a gnarled finger. "Southland will reap a whirlwind."

The joy, the hope, people making plans for hiding places if trouble came—sheds, stable, barn—and how to pack up quick if Yankees came their way. Mariah couldn't remember why she settled on the root cellar, just her worry about Dulcina. *How will she know to hide?*

* * *

Mariah marched in silence, in a fog most of the day. None of the others had much to say. Only Zeke bore a smile.

Mariah envied him his cheerfulness. In a way he was blessed. Didn't know how ugly the world could be, how much evil worked its will even in the days of jubilee. And for him, freedom was a pouch of peppermint sticks.

No large gathering around a bonfire that night. But when night took over from day, Hosea brought out his banjo. "Swing Low, Sweet Chariot," down tempo, start to finish.

Mariah was glad that Caleb didn't make himself scarce that night, but it bothered her that he was so distant. He had pitched his tent close to the one she now shared with just Zeke and the Doubles, but he didn't sup with them. Said he wasn't hungry.

"May we all sleep like Zeke tonight," said Chloe, taking a whiff of what she called nerve tea.

Like always, Mariah had tucked Zeke in early.

"Cups up." Chloe raised the dented coffee pot from the fire, began to pour into Mordecai's cup, her sister's, Mariah's.

Mariah tasted lemon balm and lavender.

Chloe handed her another cup. "Caleb could use some, I'm sure."

The tea was a brace against a howling wind. But Caleb was so silent, time so still.

Mariah tried to come up with light talk. "Is a brigade in a

regiment or is it the other way around?" she was about to ask but didn't. She knew the answer, and Caleb knew she knew.

Why is he taking Dulcina's death so hard?

When Mariah saw his fire getting low, she rose. "I'll get you some pine knots."

"Never mind," he said. "Turning in soon."

She so badly wanted to be with him, to hug him, for him to hold her. And how badly she wanted to soon be someplace safe. Safe from Rebels, Yankees, safe from another wound.

"How much longer, you reckon?" she asked.

"The march?"

"Uh-huh."

"A matter of days."

"The somewhere place still a secret?"

For the first time Caleb looked up. He shook his head. "No longer a secret."

Mariah waited, worried about Caleb getting back inside himself, shutting her out.

"Caleb?" She rubbed his arm. "What's wrong?"

"Nothing."

When eyes met eyes, Mariah held on for dear life. She saw a change come over him. She continued to stare into his eyes, continued to rub his arm. "So tell me, Caleb, where is the somewhere place?"

Caleb almost smiled. "Savannah."

"Savannah?" All Mariah knew was that Savannah was a city by the sea. "Do you know what Savannah's like?"

"Fine city, I hear," said Caleb. "Palm trees and parks, fountains, statues. Laid out orderly, in twenty-four squares. Mansions in peach and other soft colors, with porticoes, balconies. The ironwork—fences, gates, stairways, railings—some of the most magnificent in the world, they say."

Mariah knew that Caleb was coming into a better mood. He was talking whole cloth. She was overjoyed as Caleb talked on about having people there. "Well, before the war they were still there. A cousin named Isaac is a carpenter. His wife, Jane, has been running a secret school for our people for years."

"They free?"

Caleb nodded. "Quite a few in Savannah. Some you might even call prosperous."

Mariah couldn't wait! And she was so glad for some good news.

Savannah.

Sounded restful, easy, brought to mind a sweet breeze.

Mariah smiled at the sound of Savannah.

No Longer with Us

Caleb was hard pressed to take up his diary after Mariah left his tent. He lingered on the long look into her eyes. Her hand on his arm. The joy that came over her as he talked about Savannah. But as the minutes passed he could feel himself growing grim again.

The more I write now, the less I'll have to write later, he told himself. He reached for his diary, his pencil, and wrote, "Sun., Dec. 4th, 1864" at the upper right-hand corner of the page. He started with terrain.

"Sandier by the day. More clogged roads, burned bridges, thick woods. We are deep into the river-road region, mad tangle of swamps and creeks, large and small. Not many shallow. Pontoons laid down all hours. If we are not trudging through a swamp, we are up to our ankles in sand. Foraging thin. Fewer farms. We return with very little. A few sacks of sweet potatoes, a pig or 2, some chickens. Rice the only thing in abundance."

Rice and more danger.

"Reports of more than 50 deaths in Gen. Kil's cavalry in the Waynesboro battle. Rebels lost about 5 times more."

Caleb thought about the danger Mariah and other colored women on the march faced—from the men who were obliged to protect their freedom. Even though her tent was not that far away from his, Caleb had insisted on walking her to it when she decided to turn in.

Now, about an hour later, he stared at his lantern candle. For more than a minute. More than five. It was going on fifteen when Caleb felt ready to record the incident that had him all torn up.

"Dulcina is no longer with us. Same as happened to Lily. When M. came to my tent tonight I started to tell her about Lily, tell her everything, but stayed clamped up. Talked about Savannah instead. Camped near a bend in the Ogeechee River."

Dear Lord!

"Miss Chloe! Need your services!"

Mariah was sitting on a weather-beaten green cartridge crate patching a pair of Zeke's britches when Caleb called out.

Wagon load on the light side. Only a few sacks. Rice, she guessed.

And a body under a blanket.

What now?

Mariah saw Chloe roll her eyes, take a deep breath. So worn out. Mariah had spotted her trying to rub away a hitch in her hip now and then as they tended to Rachel's awful cough, prepared a compress for Hosea's back, set a soldier's broken arm. She knew Chloe had been in quite a bit of pain all day. That's why, though she herself had been feeling feverish since midday, Mariah had insisted on gathering the birch bark and leaves for a brew to treat two other soldiers suffering from the flux.

Chloe rose from the white pine crate across from Mariah. "Where's the saddlebag?" She patted her right hip.

"I'll get it," said Mariah.

She hoped it wasn't another man with a shotgun wound to the head or some part of him cut off. They had found more than a few like that. Left for dead, and Chloe unable to save them. Mariah could only speculate that the men, in one case a boy with an iron collar around his neck, had been chased down by their owners or random Rebels bound and determined to keep them from freedom.

"Found him a mile or so back," Mariah heard Caleb say as she emerged from the tent and Chloe reached the wagon. "Seems the worst of it is his—"

"Dear Lord!" Chloe gasped, stepped back.

"What's wrong?" asked Mariah. She picked up her pace, saddlebag slung over her shoulder.

Zeke scrambled up. "Mariah! Mariah!"

Mariah shooed him back. "Miss Zoe, take hold of him, please."

When Mariah reached the wagon, like Chloe, she gasped, and like Chloe, she stepped back.

CRY MERCY?

"What is it?" asked Caleb.

By then Mordecai was beside the wagon. Hagar too.

"What is it?" Caleb asked again. Mariah looked like she'd seen a ghost.

"Nero," Mordecai spat. "Mariah's no doubt told you about Nero."

"But who is he, this Nero?" asked Hagar.

"Was our driver." Mariah was trembling.

Caleb moved to her side and put an arm around her, then watched Hagar broadcast the news.

A crowd formed soon. The stamp of feet began.

"Driver! Driver! Driver!"

"String him up!" somebody shouted.

"You ain't gon' see to him, are you?" Hagar asked Chloe.

Caleb could see Chloe was in a dilemma, knew she was the

type who couldn't turn her back on a dog. "Zoe," she yelled, "boil water!"

Caleb lifted the saddlebag from Mariah's shoulder, handed it to Chloe, watched her with a rag, clearing blood from around the side of Nero's face, taking stock of the wound. He had a shoulder out of joint. A busted-up ankle too.

Mariah, arms at her sides, fists clenched, was frozen.

"How bad was he?" Hosea asked Mordecai.

Mordecai rubbed his chin, shook his head.

"The way Mariah look," said Hagar, "seems he done her a heap of harm." Hagar reached down, picked up a rock, held it out to Mariah. "Only right for you to cast the first stone."

Others reached for stones.

"Now, people!" Caleb cried out. "Let's all just calm down!" He scanned the crowd. Most in it hadn't been able to look him in the eye since they almost lynched him. Especially Hagar. "The other day," Caleb continued, "y'all came close to—"

"But we know for a fact this here man really *was* a driver!" someone shouted.

And none of them knew the half of it. Caleb imagined what was going through Mariah's mind. Reliving her father's last words—*Love you, daughter*—with the water at his chin. Remembering her mother's bloody back. Part of Caleb wished to God that he'd never come across the fiend in a ravine, never got him to come around, never practically carried him to the wagon. Part of Caleb wanted to beat the man's brains out.

"Help me!" mumbled Nero.

Mariah still hadn't moved a muscle. She only stared at Nero. Her sharp, dark eyes like knives.

Tears ran down Nero's face. "Mercy," he pleaded. "Mercy."

Mariah snapped out of her trance. "Mercy?" she shouted. "*Mercy?* You got the *nerve* to cry mercy?"

Snot dripped onto Nero's lips. "Don't let 'em do me in," he wept. "Please, Mariah. 'Member all them times I coulda, coulda had you . . . lashed?"

"I remember, Nero. I remember everything you did." Mariah pulled out her jackknife, lunged forward.

"No!" Caleb grabbed her, took the knife from her hand.

The crowd pressed closer in.

"You can't hold us all back, Caleb!" Hagar called out. "We act on Mariah's say."

"What all did he do?" needled Hagar. "Fifty stripes for every wrong!"

"You'd be whippin' till kingdom come," said Mariah.

"Jus' say the word, Mariah," Hagar intoned. "Jus' say the word!"

Caleb couldn't bear the sight of Mariah. What he saw on her face was beyond agony and rage.

She was hosting evil.

POWER

Days, weeks, months, years of misery, of terror. Days, weeks, months, years of doing other people's bidding. Days, weeks, months, years of being bypassed by mercy.

All those tears and lamentations.

For the first time in her life Mariah had power. She didn't have to contain her rage, stifle her will. For once in her life, she could do more than weep and pray.

"Look at me!" she yelled at Nero.

Nero obeyed.

Mariah relished the sight of his tear- and slobber-stained face, of his battered body. She could smell his fear and savored that.

Nero lifted a hand. It shook like he had the palsy. He raised an index finger, seeking permission to speak.

Mariah nodded.

"I done you some good turns." He swallowed. "That

night—the dungeon. Drug you away when I seen he already . . . spare you the sight of that."

"Spare me? You wretched, filthy—"

Two questions asked but never answered. Everyone on the Chaney place, the Doubles—all had pleaded ignorance, turned her mind to something else when she raised her suspicion that Nero was at the root of it all.

"Nero," Mariah said slowly. "Gonna ask you some things. You tell me the truth or I'll loose these people on you."

Nero nodded.

"What did my pa do to get the dungeon? And was it you who told Callie Chaney my ma was a conjure woman?"

Nero swallowed.

"The truth, Nero. The God's honest truth."

"I loved your mama, Mariah." Nero sighed. "After Joe pass and Judge Chaney made me head man, I thought fo' sure yo' mama be mine. Tole her as wife of a driver she get *three* dresses a year and eat mo' better."

"None of this answers my questions, Nero." The idea of her mother and Nero made Mariah sick to her stomach.

"Then yo' pa was brought to the Chaney place . . ."

"The dungeon, Nero?"

Tears streamed down his face. "I, I tole Judge Chaney he broke tools on purpose an' disrespec' me."

Mariah's hate grew hungrier by the second.

"Jus' to punish him some fo' my pain . . . Didn't know a storm was comin'."

All over again, Mariah saw herself bailing water as fast as she could.

"And did you tell Miss Callie my ma put a hex on Judge Chaney?"

"Wasn't me, I swear."

"But you're a liar, Nero. Everybody knows that." Mariah thought she now knew what it felt like to be a general. She was in charge, in command. Hagar and the others were her troops.

"I swear, Mariah, it warn't me," Nero blubbered. "Back then Miss Callie was makin' visits to that sayons woman, tryna talk wid Judge Chaney's spirit. Was sayons woman who tell Miss Callie there be evil in her house." Nero paused, took a deep breath. "I never say yo' ma did conjure. I swear to God, Mariah. I swear to God."

"What do you know of God?" Mariah yelled. She saw her young self at Miss Callie's feet, begging for mercy.

"It warn't fity," said Nero. "Times when Miss Callie had eyes on you, tree was all I whip. Didn't lay on the full fity."

The wind, whispers from the crowd, trills of birds, the crackle of campfire—all of it ceased. There was only her and Nero. And her power.

"But she died, Nero, my mama died!" Each word a gouge, a chisel. "And my—" Mariah struggled not to cry. "My brother was marked for life!"

"Miss Callie fault!" Nero whimpered. "I only done as tole!"

Mariah could no longer contain her tears. "But *you*, Nero, *you*, you set it all in motion!"

When Caleb took Mariah in his arms the tears didn't cease. When he whispered, "Don't do this—you can't do this," she sobbed harder. When Caleb tried to walk her away from the wagon, Mariah stood her ground, jerked free.

"I can do whatever I want!"

"Jus' say the word!" goaded Hagar.

Savoring her power, Mariah leaned over the wagon, got within inches of Nero's face. "You hear that, Nero? 'Jus' say the word.' All I need do is say the word, and these folks will do as told. Tear you apart."

"Tomorrow." She faced the crowd. "You'll have my decision tomorrow." Mariah wanted Nero to twist in the wind, spend the night in terror.

Monsters

Caleb followed her. Past her campsite, up an embankment.

"Mariah!"

He broke into a run. When he finally reached her, he took her in his arms, stroked her neck, and rubbed her back.

The more she cried, the tighter he held her.

"He don't deserve to live!"

Caleb held her still tighter, pulled out a handkerchief, wiped tears from her face. "Awful man, it's true."

"Awful man. That all you can say? I never told you all, Caleb. How I lived in fear of him, all the times he tried to— Caleb, he tried to take me, have his way with me! He's a monster!"

Caleb rubbed her neck, her back. "Believe me, I know what you feeling, know how much you—"

He was stunned, hurt, frightened when she pulled away. "You don't know, Caleb! Can't know! Jonah was right. You not like us. Every *second* of my life been a tightrope! A mountain of misery was Nero's doing. He don't deserve to live! No justice in that!"

"No, it ain't justice, not as humans see it." Caleb reached out to her. "But you're wrong about Nero, he—"

Mariah gave him a look that cut him to the quick.

"What?" Mariah shouted, taking a giant stride away from Caleb. "I'm wrong about Nero? Have you lost your mind?"

"What I mean is, Nero ain't the *root*. He's a branch. Say he's killed. Then what? Go back to Callie Chaney? Kill her too? Then travel back in time? How many people would need to be killed to reach the root?"

"You sayin' it ain't Nero's fault?"

"I'm—"

"He had a choice! Didn't have to—didn't have to do what he did. Because of him I lost my pa, my ma. And Zeke—if it wasn't for the bullwhip he woulda . . . been born normal. I just know it."

"What I'm saying is for your own sake, Mariah. You need to tell those people to just go about their business. Or if you want, I can tell them you said—"

The sight of her stopped him again. It was as if she wanted to scratch his eyes out. But he couldn't give up on her. Caleb walked over to Mariah, grabbed her firmly by the shoulders. "Mariah, please listen to me. For your own soul's sake, you need to tell those people to—"

It looked like her mind was going loose.

Caleb stepped back. "Do what's right—otherwise you'll never know peace of mind, of spirit."

"Peace? We in the mouth of war! Peace? Beginnin' to think it ain't possible in this world. And don't try to tell me that demon Nero don't deserve to die! It ain't right for him to go unwhipped of justice."

Caleb had an urge to tell Mariah that he knew about monsters. Monsters in others. The monster in him. He wanted to tell her about Lily, the family joy.

Tell her about seeing his sister busted up. How a simple errand in town took her across the path of a monster. Wanted to tell of the knock on the door, of Lily found in an alley, left for dead, not living long, but long enough to say who did it. A local white man Caleb knew by sight.

Yes, Caleb thought, as he watched Mariah pace and rage, he knew what it was like to burn to be the justice. He remembered that queer taste in his mouth, the fire in his belly as he bided his time, learned the man's patterns. Where he worked. Where he gambled, drank. Remembered the searing pain when his mother passed from grief. Rage became Caleb's daily bread all the more. And then came his chance for revenge.

The culprit stumbled from a tavern.

Caleb ran over, played the darkie, told him he knew where he could have a good time if he had a taste for colored girls. "Young ones," he said.

The man took the bait, followed Caleb to a bawdy street, where noise, day and night, didn't cease. Steered him to an alley, rained down blow after blow—for his sister, for his mother, for all the wrongs done to his people. Then he grabbed a brick.

Caleb wanted to tell Mariah how much he understood, then thought maybe his story wouldn't help.

Would fear?

"Mariah, Yankees won't tolerate a lynching. If you head it up, there'll be a price to pay."

"Look what happened to Dulcina. Nobody paid. Can't see Yankees bothered over a slave driver. Colored lives don't matter. And so what if I pay a price? So what?"

Caleb had one last hope. "If you loose people on Nero, and if the Yankees show them no mercy, show you no mercy . . ." Caleb stepped closer, put a hand on Mariah's shoulder.

Mariah shrugged it off. "Then what?"

"Where will that leave Zeke?"

No More!

She took off for the woods, ran blind, shattered in mind. Ran until she all but collapsed beneath a giant live oak dripping thick with Spanish moss.

Mariah sat there, behind a veil of Spanish moss, soul in civil war, fighting for some purchase on peace, but unable to cool the burning to see Nero dead.

Dusk descended.

Daylight faded.

The cloak of darkness came.

Still, Mariah sat listless, drained of tears.

On the outskirts of her mind, she heard footsteps, rustling. Soon, a crackling. Before long, warmth wafted her way.

She heard voices.

We call it the killin' stone . . . I only done as tole! . . . Jus' say the word! . . . And behold a pale horse! . . . My whitefolks was both devils . . . For your own soul's sake . . . You mine . . . Nero

ain't the root . . . *What you lookin' at, you filthy nigra?* . . . *Jus'
say the word!* . . . *Peace of mind, of spirit* . . . *Where will that
leave Zeke?*

Then she heard herself—*What do you know of God?*

She battled to believe.

"By and by all will be put right. God's watchin'." That's
what her ma had murmured the day after the dungeon.

But by and by her ma was dead too. Nothing had been put
right.

There was cannon boom, rifle fire, yet Mariah didn't flinch.
Muffled and muted too was the crackle of the fire, the squeak
of bats clustered above her head.

"Watch," Mariah muttered, coming to a cruel conclusion.
"That's all God does," she whispered. "Watch."

No more! She shook her head. *No more! No more! No more!*
Done with praying, done with hoping, with believing. Done
with God.

"Useless," she mumbled. "Nothing but useless."

But then she heard another voice.

Mariah! Mariah!

WELL?

Caleb awoke to drifting mist. In the hollow of a giant tupelo. Mariah in his arms.

He pulled his overcoat tighter around her.

She stirred.

He kissed her forehead, pressed her against his chest.

When Mariah woke up a few minutes later, Caleb saw the startle in her eyes, saw her do a double-take when she realized she was in his arms.

Caleb said nothing. Just loosed his arms. Watched her sit up, wipe away leaves, dirt, rise on wobbly legs, get her bearings, then make for camp.

Caleb followed a few feet behind.

He hung back when he saw Chloe meet Mariah halfway, hug her, and lead her over to a campfire, where Mordecai and Zoe sipped coffee and chewed on hardtack.

"Where Zeke?" asked Mariah.

"Still asleep," said Mordecai as Zoe handed Mariah a cup of coffee.

When Mariah waved it off Caleb saw her eyes were fixed on the wagon bearing Nero. Still in the same spot.

Caleb could see Nero's head bandaged. Figured Chloe had his shoulder in a sling, a splint on the bad ankle.

"Can you take me to Captain Galloway?" Mariah asked Caleb.

"What for?"

"You'll see."

As they made tracks for Captain Galloway, Caleb spotted others rising, stretching, getting their bearings, starting fires. Some eating breakfast, others staring at the dawn.

He heard scraps of conversation. About a nightmare. About the witch riding all night long. About cold in the bones.

When they reached Captain Galloway's tent, Caleb called out for him. "Captain, sir, a moment."

Captain Galloway emerged from his tent wearing his dark-blue trousers but up top only his long johns and suspenders. He had a razor in one hand and shaving cream on one side of his face. "What is it?" he asked.

Caleb looked at Mariah. She seemed tongue-tied.

"Well?" asked Captain Galloway, looking at Caleb for a clue.

Again Caleb looked at Mariah. Now he saw her strength.

Looking the captain in the eye, she asked, "Favor, sir?"

Blue Glass Beads

Mariah told Captain Galloway about the bad blood between the man ailing in the wagon and her and some others. She asked if he could get the man removed for the sake of peace.

"Not callin' for him to be cast out," she said, "but sent to colored in another part of the march."

Inside of an hour, Mariah watched Caleb driving the wagon away, with Privates Sykes and Dolan on either side, riding chestnut bays.

When the wagon was out of sight, Mariah readied herself and Zeke for the march. When they camped that evening, she was prepared to face Caleb.

"Awfully sorry for the way I acted yesterday. Sorry for yellin' at you, bein' so ugly." Instead of waiting for him to come sup with them, Mariah had brought two helpings of rice and gravy to his tent.

"No need for sorry, Mariah. Just wasn't yourself."

"But now you must think me—" She lowered her head.

"I don't think any worse of you."

Mariah looked up. "Truly?" Mariah prayed to God that Caleb was like his father. Not the changeable type.

Caleb stroked her cheek. "Really. I'm in no position to judge. Remember I told you I understood? This is why. You see . . ."

For the longest while, Mariah asked no questions, made not a sound. She just listened as Caleb told her about Lily.

"You killed that man?" Mariah interrupted when Caleb told of picking up a brick.

"Was about to when something came over me. It wasn't like I heard some still, small voice. More like I saw myself becoming a worse evil, knew if I murdered the man, his blood . . . never enough. Me, I'd never be right. I'd only soil my soul."

Mariah couldn't imagine Caleb killing a fly, let alone coming close to murder.

"Before that I used to frequent saloons, gamble, do a host of things that woulda broke my ma's heart had she known. Bad enough she couldn't get me inside a church. But after I was kept from killing that man, I put all that foolishness behind me. Set my sights on becoming a better man."

"What happened to that white man?"

"Cleaned him up. Got him into a hack. Never saw him again."

They finished their rice and gravy in silence.

Caleb was dipping their tin cups in a bucket of water when he asked, "What turned you around?"

Mariah bit her bottom lip. "I guess you could say it *was* a still, small voice."

She could see Caleb couldn't tell if she was joking or not. "Still, small voice of Zeke."

"Zeke?"

Mariah bobbed her head. "Yesterday when I went to take Miss Chloe the saddlebag, Zeke jumped up, called out to me." Tears on the rise, Mariah paused, swallowed. "He didn't call out 'Ma.' He called out 'Mariah! Mariah!'"

And the tears flowed. "Caleb, he's mastered my name." Mariah paused again to collect herself. "With all the commotion I didn't take it in. Not till later. Last night when I was drifting off." She sniffled, wiped her eyes. "Made me think maybe peace and resting easy are possible after all. Made me believe again in new tomorrows. Couldn't begin my new life with blood on my hands."

Mariah stretched her back. She wanted no more talk about the past, about pain. She wanted to talk about Savannah. "Caleb?"

"Yes?"

"What you told me the other day about your kinfolk and others in Savannah, how you know all that? How you keep in touch?"

They were still outside Caleb's tent. He'd just put more pine knots on the fire.

"By post, mostly."

"Wasn't afraid whitefolks would open your letters?"

"If they did, they wouldn't have found anything alarming. Say my cousin wrote that his wife had four new chicks, we knew Jane had four new pupils. Nothing too weighty ever went into a letter though. For that we used—mind if we continue inside?"

Mariah hesitated, then said, "Fine."

Once inside the tent, Mariah waited for Caleb to get back to the conversation. Waited while he reached for a fold-up candle lantern, a match safe, got the candle lit. Waited for him to close the tent flap. Waited for him to brush debris off his pallet. Waited for him to bid her sit down.

"For deep things we used the Kobe."

Mariah sat cross-legged on his pallet, he on the ground.

"The Kobe?" she asked. Mariah felt a tug at a memory, dismissed it.

"The Kobe is a group, but not like one with bylaws and a meeting place. Nothing like that. A secret society. Get up funds for buying folks out of slavery. Hide people who stole off. Keep our ears to the ground."

"Those in this society, they all over Georgia?"

"All over the Southland," Caleb replied. "Some free, some in slavery. Blacksmiths, carpenters, tanners, and like that." Caleb paused, then recounted his fourteenth birthday when his father told him about the Kobe. "I asked him what kind of word is that, what it meant. He said it meant to be on duty for our people."

Mariah was confused. "How did you find each other? How would you know who was a member?"

"All members have somewhere outside their house, inside their house, on their clothing, gear, or tools, a mark." He reached for his toolbox, pointed to what had always looked to Mariah like a stack of spinning whorls with a ram's horn on top.

Mariah fingered the mark. "The Kobe." She sighed, then her face lit up. "Caleb?"

"What is it?"

Mariah told him about Aunt Minda's tales and lessons. "She taught us *aban* meant strength. Her people's word for devotion was *akoben*."

"Did she now? How interesting." After a pause Caleb asked, "Did this Aunt Minda ever tell you her people's word for love?"

Mariah paused, but not because she didn't know or had forgotten. The question had her flustered. "*Eban,*" she said, avoiding Caleb's gaze. Aunt Minda said it also meant safety, protection.

The candle flickered. Mariah sat silently, wondering what Caleb would ask next.

"Speaking of devotion," he finally said, "my cousin belongs to First African Baptist—can't wait to see that church."

Mariah knew Caleb was moving into whole cloth knowledge. "Say on?" she teased. "So I can think and learn, learn and think."

Caleb smiled. "Used to be a white church and a wooden

structure. Colored bought it for fifteen hundred dollars. After a while, with the building falling apart and the congregation growing, they made up their minds to tear down the old, build anew, something to last for ages. Took four years, finally finished in '59."

"Four years to build it?"

Caleb nodded.

"Why so long?"

"Most of the work was done by bonfire and moonlight, from the bricks made down by the river to the walls made four bricks deep. Most all the ironwork, carpentry too."

"Why was so much work done at night?"

"Most of the congregation in slavery. Only allowed to work on their church in their spare time."

"Where'd the money come from in the first place?"

"Many had been saving to buy freedom. That's where the first thousand came from. The rest from a new surge of scrimping and side work."

A matter of days. That's what Caleb had said. Soon the march would be over. Even still, Mariah wished again that freedom came with wings.

"It's the church floor I can't wait to see," said Caleb.

"Fancy like marble?"

Caleb shook his head. "Wood. Here and there holes in it. In a pattern. Diamond with a cross in the center." Caleb moved the candle lantern to the side. "Never learned the meaning of the pattern, but I know the purpose of the holes."

Mariah leaned in.

"Crawlspace beneath the floor. Holes so that folks down below could breathe."

Mariah felt a shiver down her spine. "Folks who slipped off?"

Caleb nodded.

Savannah was a miracle place! Churches of their own out in the open! When he first told her about prosperous colored folks she could hardly believe it. Now she wanted to know more.

"The Pettigrews have a big brick and brownstone house. He keeps an oyster house. His wife is a top seamstress."

And there was Georgiana Kelly. "Miss Chloe will enjoy meeting her. She's a nurse."

William Cleghorn, he explained, owned a bakery on Liberty and Habersham.

"And there's Garrison Frazier. Story is he got up a thousand dollars in gold and silver to buy himself and his wife. Another minister."

"How many colored churches are there?"

"Last I knew, three, four," Caleb replied.

"I do hope your people are still there." Mariah daydreamed about stepping foot in the city by the sea.

She noticed Caleb lower his eyes. "Me too. If they are—or any of their friends—they will surely help us get our bearings, do all they can for us."

The way Caleb said "us"—Mariah wanted to hear it again. And again. "You planning to stay South?" she asked sheepishly.

"Think so."

"Wouldn't you rather head up North when the war is done?"

Caleb shook his head. "Most of our people are in the South. When the war's over and this slavery business is crushed, multitudes will need help. I want to stay and do my part."

"Let me guess." Mariah smiled. "With all that thinkin' and learnin' I bet you aim to be a teacher."

"Indirectly, you might say. Newspaper. Want to start a newspaper." After a pause, he asked, "What do you want?"

Mariah hung her head. "Nothing so grand as having a newspaper."

"A thing don't have to be grand to be good."

"There was a time I daydreamed of New York," Mariah said. She told him about her print of the African Free-School. "Had no idea how far New York was, or what I'd do once I got there." She laughed. "Now I got a hope I think I can make happen. Like I said, it's not grand." Mariah looked him in the eye. "Promise you won't laugh?"

"Promise."

"One acre. I want one acre of land somewhere safe. I want me and Zeke to be able to live off my one acre."

Mariah told Caleb about Jonah's twenty-dollar gold pieces.

"I can imagine how much you must miss him," said Caleb.

"I do, but it's all for the better. Besides, you said it's only a matter of days. How far are we from Savannah?"

"As the crow flies, twenty, twenty-five miles. Surely this terrain and Rebel devilment will slow us down some. Likely to be some Rebel resistance once we get there."

"Strong forces?"

"Captain Galloway says no."

"Any colored doctors in Savannah?"

"Don't know, but—"

"Not for me," Mariah said, seeing the alarm on his face. "I wonder if there's some special kind of doctor who might be able to make Zeke better, even if only a little."

"Well, if there's no special doctor," Caleb replied, "I promise you this. I will help you take care of Zeke." When Caleb reached for her hand, Mariah didn't flinch. "Be whatever you want me to be to him." Caleb brought her hand to his lips. "Friend." He kissed her hand. "Father. Whatever you want."

Mariah's heart raced when Caleb joined her on the pallet. She felt a quivering, a quickening, became aware of breathing heavier, of how warm his lips felt, of how good his hands felt on her face, her neck, her—

Mariah pulled away. "I should leave."

"No, you shouldn't."

"But I, I—"

"Stay."

She couldn't tear her eyes away from his. He was magnificent. "I, I, Zeke'll be—"

"The Doubles will see to him." Caleb began stroking her face again.

"I, uh—"

"Stay."

Oh God did she want to stay, but—

"All I'm asking you to do, Mariah, is stay. Nothing more." Caleb removed his hand from her face, leaned back. "This march has done wonders for my self-discipline." He laughed. Mariah burst out laughing. Both were soon laughing so hard their eyes were gleaming with tears—happy tears, love-of-life tears, love-for-the-ages tears.

When their laughter died down, Caleb took Mariah's hand. "Girl, we ain't wild dogs. You merit better than a tent on the edge of swampland. You merit a warm room, fireplace, fine clean sheets on a proper bed. And blue glass beads in your hair."

STONE OF HELP

For Wednesday, December 7, 1864, Caleb didn't start off writing about the march.

"Hardly saw M. at all today. Spent a little time with them for breakfast. In the evening I brought her a dress, a shawl, and a few other things. Also brought a high-crowned black hat to replace the one Mord. lost in crossing Buckhead Creek. Spent most of the evening at the forge."

Caleb looked at his nub of a pencil. No shaving left to do. He reached into his toolbox for a new pencil. But he didn't return to his diary. His thoughts rested on Mariah.

He dreamed of making her happy, doing all in his power to see that she never knew another hurt, another pain. He was sure she'd like Savannah. And if she didn't, they'd move to wherever suited her. If she wanted to live in New York, he'd make that happen. That's right—that's where Captain

Galloway was from. Surely he'd help them make their way in New York. And Zeke, Caleb thought. Most likely there were better doctors up North anyway.

Beside himself with anticipation, Caleb felt like the happiest man on earth!

Calm down, he told himself. *Let's first get to Savannah and see what's what.* He then returned to his diary to stabilize his mind. By writing about the march.

"Division moved at 6½. Made 7 miles. At our rear 3 skirmishes today with Rebel horsemen. 13 Yankees lost. They say Rebel soldiers have been dispatched from Augusta. All is getting worse. More fallen trees. More swamps. Sometimes 2 or 3 men needed to push wagons along. Rain this morning did not help. Nerves fraying with every mile."

And the glum and gloomy surroundings. This was an uneasy place to be.

"We have been marching among giants these days. Giant bald cypresses. Some wade in the waters, some stand on dry land, all with some of their roots jutting up. Otherwordly. Same with the giant tupelos. You could sleep three in the hollows of some trunks. And so much sound. Flying squirrels. Tree frogs. Owls. Nighthawks. Right now the wind is wailing, and this night feels too alive. Cannons in the distance."

It was past midnight, and Caleb knew he was hardly the only one still awake. He knew the pioneers were hard at work. A couple hours after they camped, a scout reported that a few miles ahead the bridge across Ebenezer Creek had been destroyed, so yet another pontoon had to be laid down. "Capt. G. has ordered me to cross with the first group in the morning to be on hand for repairs to the wagons when they reach the south bank."

Tree frogs and other creatures were getting louder. The night became a scream.

Earlier in the day, when out foraging, Sergeant Hoffmann told Caleb about the history of this desolate place. Of a town started long ago by folks from Germany fleeing some kind of hell. They named the settlement Ebenezer.

"Stone of help," Caleb wrote. "That's what Sgt. H. said Ebenezer means. The town did not prosper & folks moved to higher ground. All that's left of their first try are ruins of a redbrick church. It's across Ebenezer Creek."

Ever since the sergeant's history lesson, Caleb hadn't been able to get the hymn "Come Thou Fount of Every Blessing" out of his head.

Come, Thou fount of every blessing,
Tune my heart to sing Thy grace;
Streams of mercy, never ceasing . . .

Here I raise my Ebenezer;
Here by Thy great help I've come;
And I hope, by Thy good pleasure,
Safely to arrive at home . . .

With the night so alive Caleb figured he might not get much sleep, but given his early rise, he thought the least he could do was rest his eyes. He scribbled one last thing.

"Camped at Old Ebenezer."

FREEDOMS

Mud.

Swamp.

Tripping over tree roots.

Sloshing through streams.

Roads so snaky, narrow.

Mariah had never experienced so much stop and start on the march as she had the last two days. Stopping while wagons got righted. Stopping because of roads cluttered with slashed-down cypress trees.

And now Mariah, Zeke, and the rest, they all would have to walk today. Just as they made it to the campground last night, their wagon's front axle snapped and the front wheels fell off. Mariah knew Caleb couldn't come to the rescue. He had sent word that he needed to be at the head of the column the next morning and had camped up there overnight.

Mariah was grateful that at least her shoes were holding

up. Could be worse. So many others trudged on bare feet. She couldn't count the times she'd seen blistered feet, swollen feet, and toenails torn off. Shoes. They were the one thing Caleb always tried to rustle up. The pairs he parceled out didn't make a dent in the need.

Mariah reckoned it high noon when word spread that the work on a pontoon bridge started in the middle of the night was finally done. There was chatter, too, of skirmishes with Rebels in the rear.

"Thank God we'll be crossing soon." Mariah sighed as she summoned up the strength for another day on the march, got her sling sacks on her shoulders, her calabash canteen around her neck, then Zeke on his feet, cap tight on his head. She figured with Rebel horsemen in the rear, everybody— colored and Yankee—would move double-time as best they could. She took comfort in knowing that once they got across the creek, there'd be less to fear from the Rebels because Yankees would pull up the pontoon.

But Mariah and the others had only gotten themselves ready for another wait.

"Step aside! Step aside!" a soldier commanded.

Row after row of bluecoats marched by.

"Step aside! Step aside!"

Row after row, wagon after wagon, cattle, more bluecoats, row after row.

Cannon boom from somewhere left made everybody more anxious. Mariah guessed it was coming from the Savannah River. Gunboats.

Bluecoats. Wagons. Cattle. More cannon boom.

As Yankees passed by, the only colored marching with them were strapping-strong young men. Pioneers.

"Step aside! Step aside!"

Mariah began to panic. Never before had all the other colored been made to wait until this many Yankees marched by. Never before had they been stopped from marching behind the Yankees who had found them useful.

In vain Mariah had searched for Jonah. She had even searched for Captain Galloway, Private Sykes, Private Dolan, and Sergeant Hoffmann—any kind face.

An hour passed, another. Still waiting.

"What in creation is going on?" asked Mordecai.

"Maybe part of the bridge broke?" Chloe wondered.

"Could be Rebels ambushin' on the other side of the creek," suggested Ben.

"But then we'd hear gunfire," Mordecai pointed out.

"Maybe they makin' sneak attacks with sabers." That was Ben again.

"No," said Mariah, trying to clear the panic from her voice. "I think they makin' us wait for the whole Fourteenth Corps to cross." She racked her brains. How many soldiers did Caleb tell her were in the Fourteenth? "If I remember correctly, that's about fourteen thousand men." Now that number sounded like a world.

"I reckon we'll be here awhile." Mordecai took a deep breath and let out a loud sigh.

Dusk. Still waiting.

Just hardtack for supper in case the wait would soon be over.

It was a dry supper too. With no fresh water nearby, they only put their canteens to their lips for small sips. Mariah barely drank any water at all because Zeke was strangely thirsty, along with being fidgety, whiny. He was also spinning a lot. Mariah prayed that he wasn't coming down with whatever had Rachel's little girl in fever on and off the last two days, whatever had Miss Zoe coughing and sneezing. And Miss Chloe out of pennyroyal.

Mariah also hoped that Rachel didn't come due before they crossed. The night before Miss Chloe had said it was a matter of days, maybe hours. Rachel could barely walk, and her back was killing her.

And chilling Mariah was the sight of an old woman about to camp by herself, someone Mariah had never seen before.

Stooped but strong and the color of sweet corn, the old woman had a snakeskin around her neck. Cracked and creased leather pouches dangled from a rope around her waist. One gnarled hand gripped a walking stick fashioned from a long bone. Dimes with a hole bored through were tied around her ankles.

The woman was staring at Mariah, just like that silver-gray crane the other day. The bird looking like it was privy to a mystery.

Mariah had a bad feeling that something was wrong, or something was about to go wrong.

Under moonshine and stars. Still waiting. They took catnaps, two or three at a time.

Then came the break of dawn.

Mariah peered ahead, saw the last of the soldiers about to cross. "Get ready to move out, everybody," she said.

Gathering her things, she looked behind. For as far as she could see, hundreds, maybe thousands, of colored people, most asleep on the ground or up against a cypress or tupelo tree. Cannon boom startled them awake.

This ragtag colored regiment was soon on its feet with sacks over shoulders, bundles on heads, and maybe a walking stick—or nothing—in their hands. It brought tears to Mariah's eyes.

She looked around for the strange old lady with the long bone walking stick she'd seen the night before, but there was no sign of her.

But there was more cannon boom. A shell whizzed through the air.

Mariah looked ahead, saw Yankees moving faster across the bridge.

Another boom.

Mariah looked back, saw people rushing forward.

Something was coming. Good or—

Evil.

Mariah knew it in her bones.

Hand tight on Zeke's she prayed for wings as eagles as she, Ben, Rachel, Rose, Miriam, Mordecai, and the Doubles neared the water's edge. She felt a tightness in her chest when she saw the tramp of troops coming to an end. Only about a hundred left to cross. From the back of the last covered wagon, a pair of eyes peeked out. Praline.

Mariah looked back, saw colored crammed against each other. The air reeked of fear.

Mariah's group was within a few yards of the planked way leading to the bridge when she—they all—got a fright.

"Stand where you are!" shouted a soldier, his musket rifle at the ready. One, two, three other soldiers raised their rifles too.

Mariah stared at the soldiers in disbelief. They can't be . . .

Rachel cried out, "They gon' do what they did at Buckhead Creek! Gon' take up the bridge!"

Hagar screamed, "Good God, they can't do that!"

Mordecai shouted, "Buckhead wasn't nowhere deep as this one!"

Mariah stood there in frozen fear, staring at the black water, reckoning it to be more than a hundred feet wide, terrified at the thought of how deep.

Mariah stood there in frozen fear as the bluecoats walking backward began to pull up the bridge, with the four rifle-ready soldiers behind them, guns still trained on the people on the north bank.

"Please, no!"

"Stop!"

"Don't leave us!"

"Have mercy!"

Mariah stood with her arms around Zeke, tears streaming down her face, staring at the nothing. The nothing between Ebenezer Creek's north and south banks but water. It looked icy cold.

Then she heard the thunder—pictured a thousand horses, full gallop.

From behind more shouts and cries. One word over and over, first too faint for Mariah to make out, but it was soon a roar as people shouted it up the line.

"Secesh!"

"*Secesh*!"

"SECESH!"

Then a chorus of bloodcurdling screams.

"Help us!"

"For the love of God!"

More thunder. Could only be Rebel horsemen.

They were trapped. With no hope for Rebel mercy there was only one thing to do.

The crowd from behind surged forward, became a shove.

Bullets cracked the air.

Mariah saw Rachel grab her stomach, collapse on top of little Rose.

Saw Hosea, eyes heavenward, tears streaking down his wrinkled face. Saw Hagar drop to her knees and wail.

Saw Ben jump in.

Miriam jump in.

"Swim, Zeke, swim!"

Hand in hand with her brother, Mariah plunged into Ebenezer Creek.

Before they hit the water, she heard Zoe cry out, "We can't swim! We can't swim!"

The thunder was louder, muting the cries for help.

"Swim, Zeke, swim!"

Muted, too, the angry shouts and curses on the other side of Ebenezer Creek.

"Swim!"

Mariah caught sight of men, colored and white, hurling logs into the water, lashing branches fast together for rafts.

She heard Zeke calling out, "Mariah! Mariah!"

"Swim, Zeke, swim!"

She spotted a log, reached it, reached Zeke. "Hold on tight!"

More bullets whizzed.

She ducked. Up again she saw a pouch bobbing in the water, floating away.

"My freedoms! My freedoms!" Zeke cried out.

Then she saw him—

"No!"

Let go of the log.

"No! No, God, no!"

More rifle shots shattered the air.

She saw Zeke flailing, thrashing.

Another bullet whizzed, sent her ducking.

Up again. "Zeke!"

Down again. Couldn't see.

Up again. Couldn't see.

"Ze—"

On the Eden Road

Slumped in his tent, cup of coffee gone cold, Caleb stared at the pages of his diary. He flipped back to the entry he made the day he left Atlanta. He skimmed other pages at random. Then, for a while, he just listened to the pouring rain.

Thirty minutes had passed since he wrote in the upper right-hand corner of a new page, "Fri., Dec. 9th, 1864," then put his pencil down.

What time the division moved, how many miles marched—none of that was worth writing about. Not today. And he couldn't muster the strength to write about the crossing at Ebenezer Creek.

If only he hadn't been so far ahead.

When word reached him, Caleb had leapt onto the first available horse he saw, rode hard. But by the time he reached Ebenezer Creek all that lay upon its waters were cloaks, caps, shoes, kerchiefs, walking sticks, shawls, leather pouches, calabash canteens.

He searched among the survivors, many in huddles before fires bundled up in Yankee blankets and coats.

No Hagar.

"Mariah!"

No Hosea.

"Mariah!"

No Ben.

"Mariah!"

No Rachel, no Rose, no Miriam.

"Mariah!" Caleb called out as he stumbled from cypress tree to cypress tree, from tupelo to tupelo. "Mariah!"

"Mordecai!"

"Chloe!"

"Zoe!"

"Zeke!"

Caleb cried out until he went hoarse.

"Mariah! *Mariah!* MARIAH!"

Soon he knew that somewhere upon the waters blue glass beads floated too.

"How'd it happen?" Caleb, in a daze, asked Captain Galloway long minutes later as they sat on the banks of Ebenezer Creek.

Captain Galloway looked away, hung his head.

Caleb shook with rage. "General Reb?"

Captain Galloway nodded. "He swore a select few to secrecy, told them—" The captain swallowed.

"Told them what?"

"Told them other than pioneers to not let any colored cross."

Caleb looked up at the sky, peered at massive anvil-shaped clouds, figured there'd be rainfall soon. "Captain, can you do me a favor?"

"Anything."

"Get me attached to a man like you in the right wing. I can't ride with the Fourteenth Corps, with the left wing, no more."

"Yes, of course. I'll do that."

"Can't say what I'll do if I cross paths with General Reb."

"I understand."

Captain Galloway also vowed to write General Grant, President Lincoln, Secretary of War Stanton, and every newspaperman he knew to tell them about General Reb's infamous order.

Colored lives don't matter.

It was dusk and there Caleb sat, hollowed out and alone in his tent, when he remembered Mariah uttering those words. A tear made tracks down his cheek. And steady on was the downpour. As Caleb listened to the rain, he longed to hear her voice once more. But then he saw her. Saw her emerge from the root cellar, saw her leading Dulcina over to the scrub oak, saw her jubilant over those lace-up boots, saw her hands swimming in his buckskin gloves, saw the love in her eyes right before they kissed. His everything was gone.

Caleb did something he had not done since Lily, then his mother, died.

He wept, knowing the rainfall would drown out his sobs.

When spent, Caleb wiped his eyes, took a sip of that cold coffee, and picked up his pencil again, willing himself to write about Ebenezer Creek, telling himself that he *had* to get it all down while it was still fresh in his mind. But, in the end, all he could manage was a few words.

"Camped on the Eden Road."

EPILOGUE

Many hundred gone? Many thousand?

Not a soul would ever know nor untangle tales about what Rebel horsemen did to those who did not plunge into Ebenezer Creek.

Rife were the rumors of folks hacked to death.

Shot.

Bludgeoned.

Rampant were reports of Rebels hauling scores back into slavery.

And onward went the march.

Two more days, three, four—twelve days after Ebenezer Creek, Uncle Billy's boys took the city by the sea. And owing to the march, more than twenty thousand of Georgia's colored men and women, girls and boys, who trooped with Sherman's four corps made their great escape.

When, a few weeks later, Sherman's army quit Savannah to plunder the Carolinas, steady on a multitude marched. A host of those folks attached themselves to Captain Abel Galloway, stuck with him through the end of the war that had split America asunder, an end that came four months after Ebenezer Creek. An end with true freedom—and great hope—in its wake.

Some of those hopeful souls even followed Captain Galloway to Washington, DC, and became a part of his new mission field: a school named after a founding father and Galloway friend, General Oliver Otis Howard, "Old Prayer Book." Among the Galloway loyalists were some survivors of Ebenezer Creek.

And Jonah.

Other survivors put down roots in Savannah and surroundings, made their livings as barbers, bakers, cooks, coopers, farmers, fishermen, milliners, masons. They celebrated freedom with fish fries, barbecues, picnics. They laughed, loved, married, had children.

Caleb dropped his dream of being a newspaperman, never wrote that book, never married. He built a smithy and a home some miles shy of Savannah. Though he could have afforded one, his wasn't a large spread. Just one acre. On the Eden Road. And he called his homestead Mariah.

Year after year, on December 9, even in the pouring rain, Caleb rode out to Ebenezer Creek and tossed flowers upon the waters. Standing there alone, he saw Mariah's profile in a cloud, heard her laughter in the wind. On bright days her smile was in the sun. And year after year he recounted what happened at Ebenezer Creek to whoever would listen, whoever he thought, hoped, prayed would remember to pass the story on.

And that's how it came to be said that in a southeast Georgia swamp, when a driving rain drenches an early December day, bald cypresses seem to screech, tupelos to shriek, Ebenezer Creek to moan.

Down through the years, when science minds tried to explain it away with talk of air flow, wind waves, and such, others shook their heads. *Not so.* They said it was the ghosts of Ebenezer Creek rising, reeling, wrestling with the wind. Remembering.

Remembering desperate pleas, heartrending screams.

Remembering hope after hope, dream after dream, and body after body flowing downstream.

Mariah, who had dreamed of a long life with Caleb and at least one acre, she first remembers that twelve days before she reached Ebenezer Creek, a hungry hush sent a shiver down her spine.

Author's Note

Years ago I was invited to do a presentation in Pocantico Hills, New York. Before it, I and other authors were treated to a lovely dinner. Most of the conversation was about history. At one point, my book on Martin Luther King Jr. came up.

One host, Robert Balog, asked if King's ancestral church in Atlanta, Georgia, and other black churches carried in their name "Ebenezer" because of what happened at Ebenezer Creek.

"What happened at Ebenezer Creek?" I asked this Civil War history buff.

I knew about Sherman's March to the Sea. I knew about his vow to "make Georgia howl," and that he made good on that vow to the tune of a hundred million dollars' worth of damage.

But I had never heard about the tragedy, the betrayal at Ebenezer Creek.

During the rest of dinner, after the program, and days

later I couldn't shake the story. I wondered about the lives of those who perished in Ebenezer Creek and about the lives of those who didn't plunge in. Who did the world lose? What did the world lose?

I did a little digging. One of my first finds was an article, Edward M. Churchill's "Betrayal at Ebenezer Creek." Then in late 2010, I discovered that in the spring of that year, the Georgia Historical Society placed a marker about a mile south of Ebenezer Creek, at the end of Effingham County's Ebenezer Road. It reads:

March to the Sea: Ebenezer Creek

One mile north, on December 9, 1864, during the American Civil War, U.S. Gen. Jeff. C. Davis crossed Ebenezer Creek with his 14th Army Corps as it advanced toward Savannah during Gen. William T. Sherman's March to the Sea. Davis hastily removed the pontoon bridges over the creek, and hundreds of freed slaves following his army drowned trying to swim the swollen waters to escape the pursuing Confederates. Following a public outcry, Sec. of War Edwin Stanton met with Sherman and local black leaders in Savannah on January 12, 1865. Four days later, President Lincoln approved Sherman's Special Field Orders No. 15, confiscating over 400,000 acres

of coastal property and redistributing it to former
slaves in 40-acre tracts.

A marker can only say so much. There was no room to note
that it was from Sherman's Special Field Orders No. 15 that
the myth arose that all black people—or all once-enslaved
people—in the United States had been promised forty acres
and a mule.

There was also no room to note another betrayal: in the
fall of 1865, President Lincoln's successor, Andrew Johnson,
revoked that special order. Almost all those four hundred
thousand acres on which thousands of black people had begun
to build new tomorrows in self-governing communities went
back into the hands of ex-Confederates.

As for Secretary of War Stanton's visit to Savannah in
January 1865, before he met with General Sherman and those
black leaders—Garrison Frazier among them—he had a talk
with Sherman about Ebenezer Creek.

Stated Sherman in his memoirs: "He talked to me a great
deal about the negroes, the former slaves, and I told him of
many interesting incidents, illustrating their simple charac-
ter and faith in our arms and progress."

When the conversation turned to his general Jefferson
Davis, Sherman assured Stanton that he was a fine soldier and
that he put no credence in talk that he hated black people.

Stanton didn't let it go. He showed Sherman a newspaper

article about the incident at Ebenezer Creek. Sherman admitted only to having heard rumors about Davis taking up a bridge and leaving some black people behind. He then suggested that Stanton speak with Davis himself. When Stanton did, General Davis explained that the closer they got to Savannah the more creek-ridden the terrain, thus requiring constant use of the pontoon bridges—and Rebel cavalrymen were in hot pursuit. Yes, Davis told Stanton, at Ebenezer Creek, the bridge was taken up before all the black people crossed. But they were ones who had fallen asleep, he claimed.

And yes, said Davis, some were picked up by Confederate cavalrymen. As for Confederates killing blacks in cold blood, like Sherman, Davis dismissed that as claptrap. In a later defense of Davis, Sherman told someone that his general "took up his pontoon bridge, not because he wanted to leave them [the colored people], but because he wanted his bridge."

Jefferson Davis in Union blue survived the brief investigation into the incident at Ebenezer Creek, survived the march through the Carolinas, survived the war. He died in Chicago on November 30, 1879, at the age of fifty-one. The *New York Times* reported that he breathed his last "after being confined to his bed for five days with pneumonia." The article was titled "Gen. Jefferson C. Davis Dead. The Honorable Career of a Soldier Who Began in the Ranks—Incidents of His Life."

* * *

Jefferson C. Davis came to me out of history, as did the black people in Savannah Caleb tells Mariah about. Mariah, Caleb, Zeke, Dulcina, the Doubles, Mordecai, Jonah, and the rest, they feel to me like messengers from history. They are fictional but based on real people I have read about in books and heard of as a child during firefly nights on Southern porches and around cozy Northern kitchen tables when family lore was being served up and consumed. My characters are also based on what history tells me was possible.

Of course the journey was real.

So it is my hope that through these characters, through this book future generations will not lose sight of what happened at Ebenezer Creek, that they will remember.

And pass the story on.

RESEARCH AND SOURCES

Many sources played a key role in helping me write about the people and the places in *Crossing Ebenezer Creek*: books, diaries, and articles, which allowed me to put myself—and thus my characters—on Sherman's march and enabled me to visit the lives of black Georgians during the Civil War as well as those of Union soldiers and white Georgians. The following are chief among the sources on which I relied.

"Betrayal at Ebenezer Creek" by Edward M. Churchill (accessed from www.historynet.com).

Black Savannah, 1788–1864 by Whittington B. Johnson (Fayetteville: University of Arkansas Press, 1996).

"The Civil War Diary of James Laughlin Orr" (accessed from http://freepages.genealogy.rootsweb.ancestry.com/~jonnic /People/zUnknownConnections/Churchyard/civwdiar.html).

Cornelius C. Platter Civil War Diary, 1864–1865 (accessed from the Digital Library of Georgia, http://dlg.galileo.usg .edu/hargrett/platter/001.php).

History of the Fifty-Eighth Regiment of Indiana Volunteer Infantry based on the manuscript of Chaplain John J. Hight, compiled by Gilbert R. Storming (Princeton, IN: Press of the Clarion, 1895).

"An Indiana Doctor Marches with Sherman: The Diary of James Comfort Patten," by Robert G. Athearn, *Indiana Magazine of History* (December 1953): 405–422.

Jefferson Davis in Blue: The Life of Sherman's Relentless Warrior by Nathaniel Cheairs Hughes Jr. and Gordon D. Whitney (Baton Rouge: Louisiana State University, 2002).

Memoirs of General William T. Sherman, vol. 2 (New York: D. Appleton and Company, 1866).

Saving Savannah: The City and the Civil War by Jacqueline Jones (New York: Vintage, 2009).

Slave Life in Georgia: A Narrative of the Life, Sufferings, and Escape of John Brown edited by Louis Alexis Chamerovzow (London: n.p., 1855).

Slave Narratives: A Folk History of Slavery in the United States, produced by the Federal Writers' Project, 1936–1938, sponsored and assembled by the Library of Congress (Washington: n.p., 1941; accessed from Project Gutenberg, www.gutenberg.org).

Southern Storm: Sherman's March to the Sea by Noah Andre Trudeau (New York: HarperCollins, 2009).

The Story of the Great March: From the Diary of a Staff Officer by Brevet Major George Ward Nichols (New York: Harper & Brothers, 1865).

Three Years in the Army of the Cumberland: The Letters and Diary of Major James A. Connolly edited by Paul M. Angle (Bloomington: Indiana University Press, 1987).

"'We have Surely done a Big Work': The Diary of a Hoosier Soldier on Sherman's 'March to the Sea'" by Jeffrey L. Patrick and Robert Willey, *Indiana Magazine of History* (September 1998): 214–239.

I also drew upon knowledge acquired in writing two of my nonfiction books: *Cause: Reconstruction America, 1863–1877* (New York: Knopf, 2005) and *Emancipation Proclamation: Lincoln and the Dawn of Liberty* (New York: Abrams, 2013).

ACKNOWLEDGMENTS

Ever grateful to my first editor, Michelle Nagler, for believing that this was a story that needed to be told. And oh so grateful to my second editor, Mary Kate Castellani, who thoroughly and utterly embraced the project. Mary Kate's enthusiasm along with her wise and wondrous direction opened me up to discover things in my mind and on my heart that I didn't know were there. Thanks is also due to others in the Bloomsbury "crew": Jill Amack, Colleen Andrews, Diane Aronson, Erica Barmash, Beth Eller, Courtney Griffin, Melissa Kavonic, Linette Kim, Donna Mark, Lizzy Mason, Shaelyn McDaniel, Patricia McHugh, Emily Ritter, and Claire Stetzer. I thank you all for all your fine and so excellent work. You did so much for the book and thus did so much for me. As does my agent, Jennifer Lyons.

And, bless you, my fellow writers Joyce Hansen and Sharon

Flake. I can't thank you enough for giving the manuscript a close read and for giving me such useful feedback.

Thank you, Joseph McGill, Civil War reenactor and founder of the Slave Dwelling Project, for your read and feedback too!

Thank you, Jim Prichard, professional researcher, for reading a chunk of an early draft and for telling me about the killing stone.

Thank you, Robert Balog, for telling me about what happened at Ebenezer Creek.